Where The River Runs Deep

Also by Lynne Handy

Where the River Runs Deep

Lynne Handy

Push On Press

Published by Push On Press

Cover design: William Pack

ISBN: 978-0692953501

To my writer and poet friends who gather at the Limestone Café in Batavia, Illinois on Saturday mornings. You jumpstart my week and give sustenance to my art.

Acknowledgments

I am grateful to Laura Slivinski for her invaluable work as first reader. I am also grateful to John Arends for pulling the title out of my subconscious, to Kevin Moriarity for formatting the novel for publication, to William Pack for designing the cover, and to Annie Baldwin for taking my author photo.

Lord, how long wilt thou look on?
Rescue my soul from their destruction,
My darling from the lions.

Psalm 35:10

CHAPTER ONE

How should I characterize my mood during the winter of 2013-2014? If I were writing verse, I'd use phrases like *snow-daft* and *winter-poor*, or perhaps resurrect a word like *tristful*. My uneasy mindset made concentration difficult. Reading Federico García Lorca, whose dazzling metaphors never failed to fire my mind, I'd laze into sorrowful reflection. More modern poets, their runny angst on every page, left me alienated. I felt as frozen as the ice pond back of our townhouse.

Our. I should mention Mathieu here. Despite everything, he remains my partner. His name, along with mine, is on the mortgage. We share gas and electric bills. He launders his clothes on Saturdays, and I do mine on Mondays. More about him later.

I was speaking of my malaise.

It didn't help that I'd been forced into an outreach assignment for the university. Not to be outdone by her peers in the sociology and education departments, the dean of the English department volunteered my services to teach a poetry class at the high-medium security, all-male state prison near our town. My first walk across the prison yard with hungry eyes of sex-deprived heterosexual men on me was unnerving. I could smell their release of hormones. Heart pounding, I dashed toward the entrance. As time passed, I became somewhat inured to the weekly assault. Chin high, posture erect, eyes alert, I walked staunchly across the yard to the classroom. Inside the door, I'd breathe a sigh of relief.

Most of the inmates signed up to write poems to wives and girlfriends. Others, meaning to shock and mortify, penned odes to the turds in their toilet bowls or snot blown from their noses or corpses they'd seen rotting in alleys. Occasionally to keep order, I'd need to call for a guard.

My most serious student was Amen Hotep Jones. With regularity, he checked out poetry books from the meager library collection and brought them to class—Longfellow, Kipling, Riley, an anthology or two. After gaining approval from the EA, or education administrator, I added volumes by Angelou, Hughes, Neruda, Brooks and other more relevant poets to the collection. Lorca was banned. The EA thought Hispanic inmates might become too agitated by his descriptions of bullfights and gory deaths. While it was true the Latinos tended to pore over the works of Spanish and Central American poets, I thought his objection ridiculous. Lorca's elegies to the dead bullfighter Ignacio Sánchez Mejías were gorgeous. But one didn't argue aesthetics with the prison administration.

When I queried Amen about his name, he said his ancestors came from a city along the Nile. Though he claimed to have Kunta Kinte stories, he never shared them. I wondered if it was because I was white.

A tall thin man with a shaved head and bronze skin, Amen brought dignity into every room he entered. He was deeply spiritual and there were times, as when a robin sang outside the classroom window or sleet pelted against the panes, that we turned to listen as one person. I felt the force of his persona at those times, or perhaps, soul.

Originally from North Carolina, he wrote of rivers, red clay, and live oaks. Sometimes, the ocean. The poems I liked best were his odes to Astarte, the Middle-Eastern fertility goddess. I couldn't help but wonder if a flesh-and-blood woman had inspired his work. One of his poems I had committed to memory:

> *Velvet skin like a hound's ear.*
> *During the night*
> *did the honey bees suck your lips?*
> *Did you comb the night into your hair*
> *and is the moon your tiara?*

Amen's Astarte was many things. In other poems, he depicted her as meek as Moses, a song, a savior. So many metaphors. How could one woman possess so many traits? Perhaps she never existed, except in his mind.

The third week of class, a guard cornered me in the teacher's lounge. "You're paying a lot of attention to Inmate Jones," he said. "He's a killer. Shot a man in a liquor store robbery."

I was stunned, never dreaming Amen was a murderer.

"Don't be fooled by his 'changed man' act," he warned. "If he had a knife, he'd slit your throat. He's sly. His cell walls are covered with bible verses. Wants us to think he's saved."

Didn't Christians believe everyone was redeemable?

"How long has he been incarcerated?" I asked.

"Three years, maybe. He should have stayed down south. Got in with a gang when he moved to Chicago."

Guards had been known to lie, particularly to female employees. They feared we would come under the sway of inmates and jeopardize security. It didn't set right with me that Amen had killed. If the guard was telling the truth, I wondered if Amen had been wrongfully convicted.

* * * * *

Three weeks later, I awoke feeling wretched. Head pounding, I squinted out my bedroom window to see that a dusting of snow covered the ground. My eyes focused on a forlorn maple, its bare limbs beseeching the heavens. In an instant, the tree transformed to a trembling man, then changed back to a tree. I was left with a terrible presentiment of calamity. Swallowing a Tylenol, I dressed and drove to the prison to teach my class.

At the gate, a guard blocked my way. "Go home," he said. "The prison's on lockdown."

I tensed. "What happened?"

"Somebody got stabbed."

I remembered my vision of the trembling man. Had he been the stabbing victim?

I went home, put the heating pad on my aching head, and turned on the TV. I fell asleep, worrying about Mathieu driving on the icy roads. When he arrived home, I awakened.

"Thank god, you're all right," I said.

He knit his brows. "A psychic headache?"

I nodded. The slightest motion brought on dizziness. He made me a cup of tea and a slice of cinnamon toast, pampering me as my mother had done when I was a child.

Later that evening, the warden held a televised press conference, saying an inmate had been stabbed. He withheld identification, pending notification of kin.

"I wonder who was killed," I said.

"You're not greatly attached to anyone at the prison, are you?" asked Mathieu.

"No, but..."

There *was* Amen Jones.

That weekend I was preparing a potato and leek casserole for dinner when Mathieu peered around the corner. "Come look at the TV."

The warden appeared on the screen, looking dapper in a pinstriped suit. He identified the murdered inmate as Amen Jones, member of a Hobo gang. He'd been killed by a Latin King.

I cried out and sank onto the sofa. Amen's face appeared before me; his eyes lit with discovery, his voice hushed, savoring the words of Langston Hughes. I thought of his poetry. His talent had been nascent, but with time and study...what could he have achieved?

"Was he in your poetry class?" asked Mathieu, his eyes searching mine.

"My brightest student."

"I'm sorry, Maria."

"I don't know if he had family. He came from the south."

"Let's have an early night tonight," said Mathieu. "I'll do the dishes and then we'll go to bed. Sleep will do us both good."

The following day, I received a call from the dean. Because of Amen's murder, the university had cancelled all prison outreach programs. I put his poems in a drawer, and turned my attention to my university classes.

* * * * *

If winter had delivered the blow of Amen Jones' death, then spring, with its azure skies, budding jonquils, and leafing trees should have lightened my heart. Sadly, I found out Mathieu was having an affair with a colleague.

Originally from Togo, Mathieu taught Black Studies at the university. I taught Poetics and published a book of poems every eighteen months. We had been together for eleven years, and although I had once before questioned his loyalty, he convinced me I was in error. I wonder if I really had been.

He and I had a long-standing arrangement to lunch together on Wednesdays. I arrived at his office, thinking of tuna-cashew salad and a glass of pinot noir. As I opened the door, I found him copulating with a groaning woman who lay spread-eagled on top of his desk. Her yellow shirt was pushed over her head, rather like a felled tulip blossom. For an instant, I was unsure of what I was seeing. Was this another of my visions?

Mathieu saw me and froze. The woman yanked down her skirt and darted behind a file cabinet. The only sounds were those of my footfalls and creaking boards as I ran down the corridor, found a rest room, and vomited into the toilet.

Afterward, I realized I must have intuited his infidelity and that had been the cause of my winter angst. I moved the incident (and its ramifications) to my head, not trusting my heart to respond in my best interest. I tried to analyze the situation. Perhaps Mathieu and I went our separate ways too often. We usually had summers free, but he was interested in anthropological sites and I was always seeking inspiration, which I suppose I could have found amid the stones of Skara Brae or Machu Picchu, but I didn't enjoy rugged living. Sand in food, bug bites, and pit latrines upset my sense of well-being. While Mathieu dug for bones and treasure, I'd skip off to some lovely place replete with modern conveniences. Perhaps we were too invested in furthering our careers. Whatever the reason for our troubles, he broke my heart.

He swore to end the relationship with his inamorata, but I told him not to bother and moved into the guest room. Occasionally— after I'd drunk too much—he would tempt me into our king-sized bed. Enveloped in a boozy haze, I'd participate in what passed for lovemaking, but when it was over, when I was lying on the cold sheets, I'd remember his treachery. Disgusted with him and with myself, I'd slink back to the guest room.

I wanted to go away, to put time and space between Mathieu and me. There were a number of places I could go. Friends in London asked me to visit. My cousin invited me to accompany her to Paris. I could go to San Francisco, which I found achingly beautiful.

I could go anyplace alone.

Then I had no idea that escape would take me to the barrier islands off the Carolinas and I would meet a plainspoken man who would sweep me off my feet. Or that I would confront murders so clever they baffled the constabulary in three cities. I had no idea that I would search for and find Amen Jones' earlier writings that were both inflammatory and healing. He would live again on the outer banks and I would be there to see his rising.

CHAPTER TWO

In late March, I received a post card from Phoebe Burns, a colleague at Cherapee College on the outer banks of North Carolina. She reminded me of an email she had sent in February that I'd neglected to answer. In the email, she had queried me about teaching at the annual Daffodil Writers Retreat. The post card showed an inviting expanse of beach, calm water, and towering pines. Classes, she wrote, would be conducted outdoors in quaint gazebos.

I found the email. Retreat participants would stay in Dove Cottages, a name borrowed from the Cumbrian Lake District home of Romantic poet, William Wordsworth. A year before, I had visited the original Dove Cottage, a gathering spot for eighteenth century poets. I mused that the retreat's cottages might offer the same experience. Bonding with fellow poets appealed to me.

Bonding with anyone appealed to me.

As it happened, Mathieu planned to be in South America most of the summer. He'd signed on for a Peruvian archeological expedition. When I informed him of the retreat, he expressed relief that I'd have something interesting to do while he was away.

"I'd been worrying about you languishing here all summer," he said.

Languishing. As if my life stopped when he was gone.

The retreat seemed like an answer to a prayer. I was enticed by the notion of ocean waves, breezes from faraway lands, islands strung like rosary beads. I was thinking also of Amen Jones. He had grown up in the wilds of the Carolina coast. Hoping to find the riverside by which Astarte walked, I emailed my acceptance to Phoebe Burns.

Rilke wrote: *The smallest happening unfolds like destiny*. Amen, his poetry, the retreat—all were my destiny. I am reminded that we are part of a dynamic and unfathomable universe. We're sent where we're needed.

* * * * *

The semester ended. Mathieu packed for South America and I, for the Daffodil Writers Retreat. I flew into Norfolk on a rainy June day. Mrs. June Whitehall, a volunteer, met me in a college minivan. Dressed and hatted in sprightly peach, she helped store my luggage in the rear of the vehicle, and we began the hour-long drive to Cherapee.

As we reached the North Carolina state line, spindly pines appeared, five or six deep. Occasional gaps were wide enough to glimpse an ocean vista. Rain-smeared windows created the illusion of a Seurat painting, a pointillistic rendering of greens, grays, and blues. I was luxuriating in the view when Mrs. Whitehall's voice cut in.

"Swampland's over yonder," she said, gesturing, jingling the charms on her bracelet.

One of the Astarte poems mentioned a swamp.

> *I'll meet you in the swamp on high ground*
> *near the Big Cypress, the one with howling knees.*

Why *howling?* Did water swirl around the tree trunk, making a baying sound? Or did the poet endow the trees with human qualities? Did they symbolize the arthritic knees of slaves, buckling for masters?

"The Dismal Swamp," June Whitehall drawled, "spills over from Virginia into North Carolina. That where slaves hid out when they escaped from their plantation homes. Until he was caught, Nat Turner hid in the Dismal Swamp. You heard of Nat Turner?"

I assured her I had. I'd once written a poem about him. He had visions. His people believed he was a prophet. In 1831, he went from plantation to plantation, recruiting slaves to attack white planter families. Nearly sixty-five people were killed. Turner was caught, hanged, and skinned for his crimes.

The rain intensified. Mrs. Whitehall pulled off the highway to wait for it to lessen. While parked on the berm, she regaled me with a brief history of the area: the Cheraw Indians, Cavaliers, hard-working planters. She had finished with the War of 1812 when the rain stopped, and by the time we reached the outskirts of Cherapee, she had informed me in detail of the suffering imposed by the War of Northern Aggression. I listened politely, watching the sun break through the clouds.

She pointed seaward. "Look over there. That was once a big plantation owned by my Creighton family, God love them. Slave quarters are to the left. The big house, what's left of it, is on the right. What a shame all the great houses have come to ruin."

The house had been large. The distance between the two standing chimneys must have been several hundred feet. Four columns, two in place and two fallen, marked what remained of the grand entrance. Slave dwellings, behind the house, were a jumble of rotting logs.

My mind spun backward. I suppose you could say I time-traveled. In a vision, I saw ragged children huddled with their mother against the cold. I felt pity for them, and wanted in that moment, to reach across the centuries and liberate them.

June Whitehall's voice jarred me back to the present. "My ancestor, Peter Creighton, made a fortune in cotton and corn. He was called 'Old Peter' because he lived to be 101. I'm descended from his son, William. My family more or less kept the land together until the war I spoke of."

Still reeling from the suffering of the mother and children, I made no reply.

Ahead, a large suspension bridge glistened in the sun.

"We're crossing the Orchy River," June said. "Some Scotsman, God love him, was lonesome for the Highlands, and named the river after one he'd known at home."

I looked over the railing. The river pulsed from the mountains into the great Atlantic. Waves lifted, leaving froth. *Motion,* was the word that came to mind. *Life-giver,* another. I hoped I would have time to write a poem to the river.

We continued on for another mile before a sign indicated we had reached the outskirts of Cherapee. Buildings appeared, a gas station, a row of shabby store fronts, a café advertising barbecued shrimp. Then the handsome face of a man appeared on a billboard. It wasn't every face that could bear magnification, but his could. He had warm brown eyes, a strong straight nose, and smiling lips. His name was Luther Vance. According to the lettering, he was a native son and he was running for governor.

"Luther is kin," June said proudly, "Cherapee County is mighty proud of him."

I looked again at the face of Luther Vance. Did I see a glint of larceny in his eyes?

"Look over yonder," said June Whitehall, pointing to a section of beach framed by willows and sprawling oaks. "That's Sunfish Cove, prettiest site in the state. Some Russian billionaire wants to buy it and build a twenty-story hotel."

"Wouldn't such a structure look out of place?" I asked.

"Some think the hotel would boost the local economy."

Sunfish Cove seemed perfect just the way it was. I hoped conservationists would protect its natural beauty.

The town was spread out—a mixture of weathered brick structures, gaily-painted three-and-four-story beach houses, and stucco buildings. I'd read that the courthouse dated to the early 1700's.

A pickup truck passed. Visible through the rear window was a shotgun. We drove two more blocks. I counted three more pickups, all armed. Unused to a gun culture, I shuddered.

"You cold?" asked June.

"I'm not used to seeing so many guns."

"A couple of years ago, the legislature passed a Stand Your Ground law," she said. "Used to be, a person had a duty to retreat when an altercation arose. Now you can stand your ground if attacked in your home, vehicle, or workplace."

"How has that worked out?"

"I don't know what the statistics are regarding shootings, but I know I feel safer." She nodded toward the glove compartment. "I keep a thirty-eight handy."

I glanced warily at the glove compartment, wondering what

would happen if we hit a bump. Would the gun discharge? I was definitely in the line of fire.

We continued down Main Street to the college, a clutch of brick buildings. At the back were quaint rock-faced dwellings set in a labyrinth of hedged gardens. I assumed they were the cottage residences for retreat instructors.

June pulled the minivan into a parking spot, dodged puddles in her peach pumps, helped lift my suitcases from the trunk, and led me to a cottage near the end of the street. Two pots of geraniums rested on the small covered porch. Unlocking the door, she handed me the key and helped carry my luggage inside.

"Here you are, Professor Pell," she said. "The phone's in the bedroom. If you need housekeeping, dial zero."

She declined a tip, saying she was a volunteer, not an employee. A flurry of peach cotton, she dashed back to the minivan. I watched her go, thinking she had the same relentless energy as the Orchy River.

The cottage was comfortable, consisting of a furnished bed-sitting room, full bath, and a kitchenette with a small table and two chairs. French doors provided natural light into the sitting area where a modest stone fireplace would provide warmth in cold weather. I hung up my clothes, placed the rest in dresser drawers, and unloaded my books into a small bookcase.

A writing desk positioned beneath a white-curtained window provided a view of Cherapee Sound. Peering out, I saw three boats head out to sea, a soft wind caught in their sails. I cranked open the window, inhaled the sea air, tasted salt on my lips. Despite Mathieu's betrayal, I was determined to find peace here, working with people who loved verse.

I sat down to read *Stag's Leap*, by Sharon Olds, a collection of poems chronicling the collapse of her marriage. Her husband of thirty years found someone else. One reviewer called *Stag's Leap* "a calendar of pain." The phone rang. Lifting my eyes from a heart-wrenching stanza, I saw my own Judas was calling.

CHAPTER THREE

"I arrived in Peru yesterday," Mathieu said cheerfully. "The mountain air is unbelievably clear."

"How nice," I replied, frostily. "Have you done any digging?"

He chatted on as if we were still lovers and *she* was not with him on the dig. "We toured Machu Picchu yesterday. Tomorrow we head to our site in the valley."

"Beware of the jungle," I told him. "Snakes bite."

He was silent. I was silent. With no other options, we said good-bye. I sat staring at the walls, wishing he'd not called. He didn't understand how deeply he'd hurt me. He never would. Perhaps empathy was reserved for civilized people. How civilized was Mathieu? Only two generations ago, his family had paraded around the jungle with feathers covering their loins. As for his lover's presence on the dig, he'd said he could do nothing about it. She'd been accepted before he had been.

"You could stay home," I'd said.

He had stared at me as if I'd lost my mind. "And miss the opportunity to study with Dr. Wachowski?"

To Mathieu's credit, Dr. Paul Wachowski was a noted archeologist, specializing in South American artifacts. He was elderly. Digs were arduous undertakings. This could well be his last trip into the Peruvian jungles.

Needing to distract myself from thoughts of the man with whom I'd spent the last eleven years of my life, I changed into jeans, sweatshirt, and sneakers, and went outside. At the same time, my neighbor opened his door. I recognized him.

"Bo Bennett!" I cried. "I didn't know you were coming."

He ran long, lean fingers through thick, red hair. "Maria! I came on short notice. I'm subbing for someone who got sick."

Bo, born Bonnie, loped over to greet me. We'd been undergraduates together at a small Indiana religious college and had kept in touch with Christmas and birthday cards. Over the years, Bonnie had transitioned to Bo, and now it seemed the change was complete, for he looked like a rangy, sensitive man, rather than the awkward female he had been. He had an abrasion on his forehead.

"What happened to your head?" I asked.

"I was poking around a mausoleum in a cemetery, and a piece of masonry fell off and conked me."

"What were you doing in a cemetery?"

"Researching my next book. I'm doing a history of the Creighton family. Peter Creighton secured a land grant and migrated here in the late 1600's. The ruins of his plantation are just outside town. The retreat invitation was timely."

Bo was drawn to historical sagas. His last book had been a well-acclaimed biography of Francis Marion, the Swamp Fox.

"I drove past the Creighton ruins," I said. "My driver said she was a descendant."

"He has lots of descendants." Bo lowered his voice. "Some met mysterious ends. A year ago, Dorothy Creighton, Old Peter's ninth great-granddaughter, was stabbed in the neck with gardening shears in St. Petersburg. Six months later, her second cousin, Monty Dodd, was shot dead in his home in Atlanta. Something's afoot. I haven't figured it out yet."

"The murders could be coincidence."

"Maybe, but more may have been murdered. I'm looking into recent Creighton deaths."

I frowned. "If Peter lived in the 1600's and had several children, there could be hundreds of living descendants by now. How on earth can you track them all down?"

He stared at me. "There's a worm somewhere, something rotten. Did I say the Creighton graves have been desecrated?"

"No."

"Last Christmas Eve, tombstones were toppled and spray-painted. Vandals must have loosened the piece of frieze that fell on my head."

"Do the police know who vandalized the graves?"

"I talked to the sheriff. Not a clue."

It began to rain again. Bo looked at his watch.

"We're supposed to meet for drinks at the bar," he said. "Come on. I know where it is."

He grabbed my hand, and we hurried up a wooden walk and into a mustard-colored shack with a livid green sign: Ye Olde Tuckaway. From the jukebox, a tenor sang longingly about his hometown. Red and green linoleum, columbine-patterned, covered the floor. A few people stood at the bar. Bo said they were a mix of instructors and students. I recognized three poets and waved. June Whitehall filled a pretzel bowl while chatting with an elderly gentleman.

"Maria Pell!" cried a familiar voice, "I've been looking for you."

Phoebe Burns, the colleague who had invited me to the retreat, ran to embrace me.

I told her I'd just arrived. She and Bo knew each other and we all sat down at a corner table. A waitress in a checkered apron took our orders and came back with our drinks.

"Ready for tomorrow's classes?" Phoebe asked.

I sipped my margarita. "As ready as I'll ever be."

Phoebe beamed at a group gathering around a long table at the end of the room. "Our students," she said. "Which of them will go on to win a Nobel Prize?"

The group was predominantly female, ranging in age from early twenties to middle-age. A few men stood together, looking for places to sit. Some of the women wore jeans and T-shirts; others, colorful sundresses.

An older woman with shoulder-length silver hair strode in and sat down at the students' table. She wore harlequin glasses, a cobalt blue maxi dress, and jeweled sandals. She had the kind of bearing that changed the balance in a room when she walked in.

"Who's that?" I asked.

"Lavinia Creighton Dawson," said Phoebe. "She's president of Cherapee College. She sits in on all the retreat sessions and has input about who comes back next year."

President Dawson held a black notebook in one hand, and in the other, a green pen. She was writing. I'd be worried if that black notebook came out when she visited my class. She dropped her pen. It rolled downhill, coming to a stop by the snowy-white sneaker toe of a young African-American man. He looked down at the pen.

It seemed to me that conversation stopped, although I don't think it really did. June Whitehall stood, hands on hips, watching. My shoulders stiffened, picking up on tensions in the room. It would have been a simple act of kindness for the young man to pick up the pen and hand it to Lavinia Dawson, but he didn't. President Dawson apparently knew he wouldn't, so retrieved it herself. The young man got to his feet and left. My eyes followed him. At the entrance, he high-fived a girl, as they looked toward Lavinia Dawson. I took a deep breath. Race tension was alive in Cherapee County.

As Mathieu's partner, I was familiar with racial tensions. Black women looked at me with resentment because I had snatched one of their handsome, educated brothers. White people, outside my group of friends and acquaintances, stared, wondered.

Bo touched my arm. "I see a friend standing at the bar. I'm going to speak to him."

Phoebe and I leaned in to gossip over drinks for a half hour, then linked arms to head for the banquet hall, where dinner was to be served. We crossed a stretch of campus on a brick walk. A slight breeze swayed lantern lights. Shadows moved.

As we walked between buildings, Phoebe said, "I'm sure you noticed the high-five at the door. The boy is Lanny Faire. He has no reason to be kind to Lavinia. She sold land the Faires had worked since Emancipation. The new owner leveled the houses and brought in herds of goats. Wasn't only the Faires that lost their land—so did several other families." Phoebe slid her eyes at me. "Lavinia probably thought nothing of it. She's descended from the old aristocracy. *Let them eat cake* mentality, you know."

Did I hear a false note in Phoebe's explanation for Lanny Faire's behavior? I thought so. She didn't want me to know there was racial uneasiness in Cherapee County.

A fog horn droned as mists unfurled from the Sound. A water bird shrieked. Windows were shuttered—a reminder that the area was located in a hurricane zone. Phoebe and I passed the music hall, then stopped at the culinary arts building.

"Here we are," said Phoebe. "I hope you'll love your time at the Daffodils Writers Retreat so you'll want to come back next year."

"President Dawson might not approve of my teaching technique," I said, only half jesting.

"Oh pooh, Maria. I've audited your classes. You're a great teacher."

She kissed my cheek. "I have to help June Whitehall with arrangements. Find your place card. I think you're seated next to the head table."

I did as she suggested, found my place card, and sat down with others at a long table with centerpieces of white orchids and pine boughs. A printed menu lay atop my bread plate: fried soft-shell crabmeat over Brussels sprouts and tomato slaw, long-grained rice, and hush puppies. My mouth watered.

Students began to serve the food. I tasted the crab. Magnificent! My dining companions murmured appreciatively as their taste buds responded to the creative pairing of shellfish and sprouts. Did I taste bleu cheese in the dish? I glanced at President Dawson. She had been served a small steak. Was she allergic to shellfish?

On my right was a poet named Hal from New York City. Jade English, a short story writer, sat on my left. As we ate, we discussed methods to jump start our work. Hal relied on prompts, often supplied by his three-year-old daughter. Jade used free-writing. I heard my poems forming and wrote them down. Sometimes I used index cards to plan segments.

When we finished our meal, servers brought in a four-layered Lane cake, glistening with a coconut, pecan, maraschino cherry glaze. Though my portion was thin, it must have contained at least two thousand calories.

June Whitehall banged a spoon on a glass. "Before you partake of your yummy sweet," she said, "I must tell you its history."

She went on to say that an Alabama native had created the cake for a nineteenth century contest. "This is a prime example of our exquisite southern cuisine. Paired with the wine your servers are now pouring, you have in store a rare gastronomical experience. Bon appetite!"

She sat down and cut into her cake.

Though delicious, the cake was very rich, and I ate only one forkful. Stunned by the surfeit of food, my companions and I lingered at table, discussing the following day's activities. Then people began moving around. My poet acquaintances came over and we briefly discussed our courses. One was focusing on Shakespearian sonnets, another on the English Romantic poets. I was teaching postmodern poets.

Bo Bennett sought me out and we walked back to our cottages, chatting about the evening. He had met some of his students and was pleased by their enthusiasm. Before entering his cottage, he opened the trunk of his car, and removed two binders and a book of cryptogram puzzles.

"Research and recreation," he explained.

I smiled, remembering the younger Bo and his devotion to puzzles. We said goodnight. I went inside my cottage and looked at the work on my desk. I hadn't remembered placing Amen Jones's Astarte poems on top of my notebook, but there they were. Absent minded, I told myself. I laid out my clothes for the next day, opened the window to let in the sea air, climbed in bed, and snuggled under a lavender duvet.

CHAPTER FOUR

The following morning, the sun was out, and I walked to the college cafeteria for breakfast. One of the servers instantly caught my eye—a tall, copper-skinned beauty serving fruit compote. Her nametag read *Goddess*. At first, I thought it was the name of the service company, but while waiting for my cheese omelet, a white-aproned older woman called to her, "Goddess, can you open this jar of marmalade? My arthritis is giving me fits today."

The young woman went to the kitchen. While spooning chopped green onions on my eggs, I saw her return. She *did* look like a goddess. She must have felt my gaze, for she suddenly turned in my direction and impaled me with piercing brown eyes. I looked away. Jade English called to me and I joined her table.

At 8:30, I strolled down the path to my gazebo classroom near the Sound. My students numbered sixteen and were mostly young. A clean-shaven man and two women—one with blazing red hair—were older.

"Good morning, Daffodils," I said, smiling. "I'm your instructor, Maria Pell. I'm delighted to leave the constraints of a university classroom and come to this lovely outdoor setting. I'd like to ask why you're here and what you hope to get out of this summer program."

Some hemmed and hawed, surprised by the question, but all responded.

"I want to write well enough to be published," said the redhead.

"Theory," said another. "I want to understand the theory of poetics."

From the older man: "Someone said my poetry was out-of-date. I want to write relevant verse."

As I went around the gazebo collecting answers, I hoped to help my students achieve their goals. They would be offering work for critiquing, which could result in hurt feelings. At the beginning of each course, it was my habit to present an awkward draft of my own work for them to analyze, so I could model how to receive criticism.

I read "November Rose."

> *Speak to me, pink flower,*
> *Here today, gone tomorrow.*
> *A snip of frost, then tossed*
> *Into a mulch of leaves,*
> *Drained of color,*
> *Soggy from rain.*

"Help me with this poem," I said. "First, tell me what's right with it, then, what needs work."

Someone liked *snip of frost, then tossed.*

Then they took the poem apart. The redhead thought the poem was trite and maudlin. The older man said it reminded him of Tennyson.

"It didn't have enough momentum for you to finish it," said a young woman, "so maybe you should just pitch it."

Others agreed. I thanked them for their honesty, having perfectly modeled receiving criticism.

We moved on to a discussion of "Ode to Thought," by Sharon Olds. My students were a good group, working together, responsive to suggestion. As I listened to their comments, Lavinia Dawson slipped into a seat near the entrance, and took out her black notebook and green pen. Uh-oh, I thought. When the session ended, she walked over to me.

"Your students are certainly motivated," she said.

"Sharon Olds does that to people," I replied.

I watched her walk away, shoulders back, chin lifted, making much of her descent from Old South forbears. Why had she dislocated the Faires and other families from her land? A need for funds? How much was she paid as president of the college? Surely, she drew a six-figure salary.

Gathering my papers, I took the path back to campus. Emerging from the shrubbery, I saw Goddess speaking on her cell phone. She still wore her blue apron from the cafeteria.

"This is Goddess Jones," she said. "I'm calling about the car you have for sale."

Jones. I stopped in my tracks. Was Goddess kin to Amen? Was she the Astarte of his poems?

* * * * *

On my way home, I stopped at a small grocery and bought food. I turned on my laptop when I entered my cottage and checked for email messages. There was one from Mathieu, saying he'd watched a demonstration of Incan pottery-making, and another from a friend, asking for advice on whether to purchase a beagle or a German shorthair puppy. I didn't answer Mathieu's message, but advised the friend to get the beagle. I'd heard they were merry little dogs.

Bo knocked on the door just as I finished a ham and cheese sandwich.

"Do you want to go to the cemetery with me?" he asked. "I'm looking for the death date of one of Old Peter's wives."

Interested in the vandalism he'd mentioned, I put the mustard jar in the refrigerator and joined him. Though he had a car, we decided to walk, sticking to the sidewalk bordering the highway until it thinned to a path.

"Look at those live oaks," I said pointing to a trio of low-limbed, sprawling trees.

"Perfect for kids to climb on," he said.

"Why are southern trees so gothic? Think of the Spanish moss, the loblolly pines."

"I think it's the way they're named. Southerners have a way of naming things."

"Are you saying they have more imagination than northerners?"

He didn't answer. We had come to the Orchy River and he paused to look at the dark roiling water. *Unfathomable*, I thought, like the country it passed through.

"I wonder what's at the bottom," he said.

"Rotted ships from the Revolutionary and Civil wars?"

"Old bones gnawed by the fishes?"

"Why did you say that?" I asked.

He shrugged. We turned west, following the river's course.

"There's the cemetery," said Bo, indicating a tall iron fence, overgrown with ivy.

Shading my eyes from the sun, I gazed at the old cemetery, guessing it to be about a mile from the Sound, but only a few hundred feet from the river. A heron flew by. A rodent swished through the grasses.

Then suddenly, a dark aura rose over the graveyard like a malevolent rainbow. Since the dead had no energy to radiate, I could only reason that some of the people buried there had not found peace. I opened my mouth to tell Bo, but he was already at the gate, pulling it open.

"Come on, Maria," he said. "I'll show you the Creighton graves."

I headed up a rise stippled with white clover. A gravel road curved to the gates, then narrowed. The berm bore the imprint of tires. The older section, just inside the gates, consisted of tilted stones and statues of weeping women in trailing robes. Breathless, I stepped into the past. Headstones were made from fieldstone and granite; some cut thick to stand for centuries, and some thin as wooden laths. Great willows drooped over the graves. Kudzu hung from maples and oaks. Children's headstones were adorned with reclining lambs. Walking with Bo toward the Creighton plots, I heard the silence of desolation.

Here lie the unforgiven.

Here lie the slave owners.

Bo halted. "This is where the Creightons are buried," he said.

I snapped to attention. To my left was a granite mausoleum sculpted with oak leaves and kneeling angels. Black spray paint covered half the structure. Though efforts had been made to remove the paint, I could make out the words *Killer* and *Fiend*. Damage to headstones surrounding the crypt was more substantial. Some had been toppled, some crushed.

"Whoever did this was filled with rage," I said.

"The sheriff said he found footprints," commented Bo. "Couldn't match anyone to them."

"According to Phoebe, Lavinia Dawson sold land people had been living on for generations. I wonder if that had anything to do with defacing the graves."

Bo didn't answer. He was bent over a headstone, peering at an inscription.

My skin began to tingle. What grievance caused this rage? The bone-thin slave mother and children edged into my mind. Was the vandalism connected to the Creightons' slave past?

Bo found the death date he was looking for and we returned to our cottages via the river path. Evening fell and I realized I was hungry. I'd bought only sandwich fixings from the grocery, and wanted something more substantial, so I headed toward Main Street, hoping to run into people I knew. As it turned out, I saw none of my writer acquaintances and stopped in at a café.

The dining area was filled with a mix of races. Two Asian couples were seated in a corner, and I wondered if they were connected to the college. The receptionist showed me to a table near the window. I took a chair where I could see into the room. A woman laughed; it was a distinctive laugh, like the joyful pealing of bells. Turning, I saw Goddess Jones sitting at the table with the young man who'd refused to pick up Lavinia Dawson's pen. Instantly, I thought of Amen Jones' poem:

> I behold you, woman of clay
> Your laughter is an aria of joy.

I couldn't remember the rest. Under the pretense of moving my chair so I could see out the window, I positioned myself to better view Goddess. She wore a yellow sundress and matching sandals. Her nails were painted teal blue. She was engaged in animated conversation with her companion. They resembled each other. Were they brother and sister?

How I was tempted to go to the table and ask if she knew Amen! But I didn't. He was so recently dead. If she was the Astarte of the poems, she might be grieving.

Goddess and the young man finished their meals and left. As a blonde waitress cleared the table, I heard her mutter, "Cleaning up after niggers."

Use of the n-word startled me. In my circles, it was never heard. The waitress felt the heat of my stare and ducked her chin to look at me. I met her gaze. She scowled and left, balancing a tray of dirty dishes. I paid my bill, hurried home. The night made me feel anxious. I double-checked the locks on my doors before retiring.

* * * * *

I woke to an Elizabeth Bishop morning: *This celestial seascape, with white herons got up as angels, flying as high as they want and as far as they want.* After eating a light breakfast, I hurried to the gazebo. I had promised to read from one of my favorite poets and had asked my students to do the same. I thought I'd read from Bishop, whose elegant way with words never failed to sooth me.

At ten o'clock, people trickled in, took their seats, and looked at me expectantly.

"It's Elizabeth Bishop today," I said. "Let me read her last poem, "Pink Dog."

As I read the poem, which described poverty in the mist of Rio's carnival, several pairs of eyes lit up, recognizing that the dog metaphor took on additional meaning.

"How'd Bishop do that?" asked the red-headed woman.

"Very carefully," I answered. "She was attentive to nuance."

The class read from their favorite poets, which tended to be post-modernists like Levertov, Baraka, and Padgett. Two of the older students read from Blake and Wordsworth. Just before noon, I dismissed class and gathered up my papers.

On my way home, a cocker spaniel puppy darted out into the street. Fortunately, no cars were coming. I looked around for its owner and saw no one. The pup could have been no more than two or three months old. Setting my briefcase on the sidewalk, I scooped him up. He wriggled free and headed down an alley. I followed. A woman in a white dress picked up the puppy, snapped on its leash, and headed in the opposite direction.

I looked up and found myself standing under a sign for the local newspaper: The Cherapee Sun. If Amen Hotep Jones was from Cherapee County, the local newspaper might have published his obituary. I went inside.

An elderly woman sat behind the front desk. I inquired about Amen's obituary, saying he died last February. She clicked on her computer.

"I knew Amen," she said. "He went to see a relative up north and was killed by a gang. Such a shame. He was well-liked, a hard worker."

She seemed not to have known he was killed in prison.

"Here it is," she said. "Do you want me to print if off?"

"Yes, please."

"It'll cost you five dollars."

I reached in my purse, extracted a five-dollar bill, laid it on her desk. She walked slowly to the printer and came back with Amen's obituary. I went outside to read it.

Amen Jones 1974-2014

Cherapee County native Amen Hotep Jones was laid to rest on February 20, 2014 in the Cherapee Cemetery. Amen was born on June 5, 1974 in Cherapee to Horus and Gracelyn Jones, and died on a visit to Chicago, IL. He farmed some of the Creighton land near county road 12 and Marsh Center. He is survived by his widow, Alberta, and two step-sons.

Darn! Goddess wasn't his wife. Someone named Alberta was. I hurried back inside the newspaper office.

"Excuse me," I said to the old woman, "do you know how I can contact Amen's widow, Alberta?"

"She works at the college cafeteria," she responded. "Only don't ask for Alberta. Nobody calls her that. Ask for Goddess."

I smiled. Now I knew Goddess had to be Astarte! I thanked the woman and slid the obituary into my briefcase. As I resumed my walk home, I realized Amen was buried in the same cemetery Bo was searching for historical information about the Creighton family.

How should I approach Goddess? She might be sensitive to the fact I knew Amen had been incarcerated. I puzzled over the quandary.

That evening, Bo invited me to accompany him to the cemetery again. We took flashlights, not trusting the light to hold for our return journey. I told him the story of Amen Hotep Jones and said I'd like to search for his grave.

"He was black? Then he's buried in the colored section. I'll show you where it is."

We took the same path to the graveyard, and paused alongside the Orchy to watch the fierce river currents crash against the rocks.

"The tides affect the flow," observed Bo.

The river is an artery, I thought, putting words together to use in a poem: *turbulence, pounding, erratic.*

"I see storm clouds on the coast," interrupted Bo. "We should hurry. There's a pavilion near the entrance in case we get caught in the rain."

We hurried on, reaching the pavilion just before the downpour, which lasted only a few minutes. A pall still lay over the cemetery. *Bad blood.* The words came to me as Bo and I ventured onto the walk leading to the Creighton graves. This time, he was searching the headstones for William Creighton's wife. My head was bent, looking too.

I heard footfalls.

Goddess Jones glided past, carrying a vase of roses. She either didn't see or ignored us. Her eyes were focused ahead. Wherever she went, she didn't linger, for she soon retraced her steps in the opposite direction.

I was certain she had visited Amen's grave. Leaving Bo talking into his recorder, I went to see where she had left the flowers. Heading downhill, I passed a stone chapel. The grass grew sparser, the vines tangled in my hair.

I came to a wire fence. On the other side, the headstones were small or nonexistent, and I knew I'd come to the colored section. The rusted iron gate creaked open as I unlatched it. I began to walk between rows of graves. Light grew dim as I came to the end of a row and I switched on my flashlight and turned to go down the next. Back and forth, I swung the flashlight. A small animal rushed past me. I felt its fur against my ankle and jumped. A night bird shrieked. Then I tripped over a root and fell. The flashlight landed on the ground, its beam illuminating a vase of roses. Scrambling to my feet, I picked up the flashlight and shone it on the metal marker: Amen Hotep Jones 1974-2014.

Silently, I paid my respects to Amen. Breezes chafed the pine boughs. My hair lifted from my neck to swish over my face and I brushed it back with my hand. I heard a distant roll of thunder.

> *Thunder rides*
> *In a chariot of fire.*
> *Raven man dies*
> *In a whirlwind*
> *Save me, Astarte.*

One of the Astarte poems. After reading it, I'd asked Amen if he was referencing the prophet Elijah's death. In 2 Kings, Elijah was taken in a whirlwind to Heaven after a flaming chariot and horses appeared. Amen had said he'd been thoroughly "churched" in his youth, and often used biblical references, but for this poem, he'd been inspired by a thunderstorm over the ocean. He'd used *Raven-man* to depict natural man.

"The appeal to Astarte?" I'd asked.

"My muse."

Of course, I'd guessed Astarte was his muse, but I was after the name of a flesh and blood woman! Was that woman his wife, Goddess Jones?

When I returned to the Creighton burial plots, Bo had company. Lavinia Dawson and June Whitehall had joined him. I eavesdropped.

"I sent a handyman to clean up this mess," Lavinia Dawson said, lifting a lantern to better view the damage. "I see he hasn't finished."

Bo scratched his head. "Who do you think did this?"

"I have my eye on that Lanny Faire," said June.

"The sheriff said there were few clues to go on," Lavinia said. "Someone saw a car parked behind the chapel."

"A car?" said June. "I didn't hear about that."

"Yes, a car," repeated Lavinia. "With local plates. But the witness didn't get the number"

"Who was the witness?" asked June.

"I don't remember." Lavinia surveyed the damage done to the headstones. "This mess has to be cleaned up before the reunion. Creightons gather here every July to honor family. The reunion lasts for two days. Kinfolk come from far and wide, and fill the motels and bed and breakfasts for miles around. Last time, two hundred people attended."

Bo's eyes widened in alarm. I read his mind. If someone was killing Creightons, the reunion would be the perfect place to do it.

Lavinia touched Peter Creighton's defaced name plaque. "Such disrespect. Old Peter must be rolling in his grave." She turned to Bo. "He was the sixth son of a Scottish earl. Laws of primogeniture forced him into the world to seek his fortune."

"He wasn't penniless," countered Bo. "He came on a headright grant financed by his uncle."

"You've done your research," Lavinia said. "After he built a house, he sent to Glasgow for his wife, Emma. She was his first wife. After Emma, there were Constance and Mercy, also Glaswegians. Emma and Constance died in childbirth."

"Emma gave him four children," said Bo. "Three sons and a daughter."

Lavinia corrected him. "Only sons. There was no daughter." She took a few steps away from Bo. "I'm not sure I want you to write about my ancestor, Mr. Bennett. You need a feel for the history of the times. I don't think an outsider can weigh the good and the bad, and come up with an accurate account."

"Are you referring to the shackles in the old slave houses?" asked Bo.

A pained expression crossed Lavinia's face. "People of means had slaves. It wasn't the worst thing..."

"How else to work the land?" asked June.

"The executions..."

June bristled. "There were ghastly slave uprisings. Why, those n...slaves were killing white babies in their beds! We can't sit around and let the darkies kill us."

How easily June Whitehall slipped into the present tense!

Lavinia broke in. "Cousin Luther is running for governor, Mr. Bennett. I hope publication of your book will come after the election."

Bo didn't answer. I cleared my throat and stepped out from the trees.

"Professor Pell," Lavinia said, drawing out the vowel in my surname, "you startled me."

"I've been walking in the graveyard," I said.

"What a peculiar thing to do," said June. "You could fall over a root and hurt yourself."

My appearance ended discussion of Bo's book. Lavinia swung her lantern for a final view of the graves. "Let's go," she said. "It's getting late."

The women made their way down the hill. Before they were out of earshot, I heard June say the words, *Sunset Cove*, and remembered the beach and magnificent live oaks on the outskirts of Cherapee. Lavinia replied in an angry tone. Did the women disagree on the sale to the Russian billionaire?

Bo was still thinking of his book. "I'd hoped Lavinia Dawson would cooperate."

"Perhaps you can convince Lavinia that you need her help to establish that balance of good and bad she mentioned," I suggested.

Bo looked dubious. "Hard to find much good in the early Creightons. They were brutal in the way they ran their plantations. Read *The Annals of Cherapee County*. I've a copy in my cottage, if you're interested."

I was interested, but when we returned to the cottages, Bo's copy of the *Annals* was missing.

"I know I left it on my desk," he said, shifting papers. "What could I have done with it?"

His door hadn't been locked. "Maybe someone stole it," I said.

"It was a library book. The librarian will be upset if I don't return it."

We turned the cottage upside down looking for the book, but it wasn't there.

"Didn't I read that Cherapee County has a historical society?" I asked. "Surely, they will have copies of the book."

"That's still not going to help me out with the college librarian," Bo fussed.

"Perhaps the book will turn up," I said, patting his arm.

* * * * *

After class the following afternoon, I walked down to the Orchy, still working on my river poem. I thought I had my first line: *Flash of stone and froth.* Bo was standing disconsolately beside a nest of pines. He'd had no luck finding a copy of the *Annals* at the historical society library.

"Their copies were all missing, too," he said.

How curious, I thought. Was someone trying to steal Cherapee County's past?

"Tell me what the *Annals* said about the Creightons."

He walked down to the shore, tossed a pebble into the rushing water. "Many early colonists were sons of Celtic chieftains, who administered justice within the borders of their fiefdoms. Their sons continued that practice when they immigrated. Old Peter was no exception." He glanced at me, then added, "Plantations were far apart and people couldn't spy on each other."

Not like the inhabitants of New England villages.

He stared past me. "Justice was perverted and desperate. Planters burned their slaves alive for the slightest infraction. Whites drank a lot of rum—if that's a defense."

Bo must have noticed the bleak expression that crossed my face. "Remember the times," he said quickly. "In England, they were drawing and quartering people. Crowds came to watch."

He pointed to a section of land that jutted out from the trees. "The Creightons carried out executions not far from where we're standing."

Then the air grew close. The afternoon sun ignited the yellow sand. The river caught its glints and in some spots, light sparked from the waves. A southerly ring of pines groped for the sky. In an instant, I was caught in thrall to a time when a merciless human drama played out. A stake made from a thick pine protruded from a hole dug in the sand. Sweating white men dragged a black man up a scaffold. His wrists were bound behind his back. The men pushed him knee-deep into a nest of briars and lashed him to the stake. They torched the briars, piled on wood, and rejoiced in his screams. Voices keened. Flames leapt as high as the roof of a nearby shed. The burning man screamed to an African god to save him. Dante could not have conjured such a scene: crackling wood, the stench of burning flesh, the terrible sound of suffering.

As I backed away from the unholy scene, I saw a white man sitting on the verandah, holding a whiskey glass. Beside him, a woman wept. "Now Constance," he said, "it's no different than roasting a goat."

His amber eyes glowed in the firelight. I thought I was looking at the devil. I grabbed Bo's arm to steady myself.

"What's wrong?" he asked.

I struggled to speak. "I saw it played out. My god!"

"You were imagining it?"

"No, I saw it. A vision..."

I had stepped back in time to the night of the execution. Few people knew I could time travel or that I communed with the dead. I'd never had occasion to tell Bo.

"You saw an execution? Here, on this spot?"

My voice was hoarse. "Yes, yes, it was dreadful. Weren't there laws regarding treatment of slaves?"

"They were property—like livestock," He answered impatiently. "Tell me about this vision."

"I can't. Not now. It takes too much out of me."

Whose execution had I witnessed? And what had the unfortunate man done? Did the defiled graves have something to do with the Creightons' savage treatment of their slaves? Was that Old Peter I saw on the verandah? Could the thirst for vengeance live for four hundred years? I thought of the Middle East, where hatred was passed from generation to generation.

Of course, it could.

Thoughts tormented me as Bo and I walked down the hill. As we departed the park, a tall, thin woman with wild black hair stood by the side of the road, waving a stick.

"Fakers! Hypocrites!" she shouted. "Thieves!"

"Who is that?" I asked Bo.

He didn't know. "She's obviously drunk," he said. "Somebody should take that stick away from her."

As we hurried away, I looked back like Lot's wife and wished I hadn't. The woman looked like an ancient *baobhan sith*, a hag-like creature in Scottish folklore, foretelling death.

CHAPTER FIVE

Mathieu called before I went to bed, sharing news of shards he'd unearthed at the dig. He was excited at the find.

"Etchings show people at work," he exclaimed, "cutting fronds, catching fish, attaching spear heads. What a reverence the potter showed for industry!"

"Capitalism at work," I said.

"Um, yes," he said.

Why did he continue to call me? I'd made it clear that I no longer trusted him. For nearly twenty minutes, we discussed what the etchings could mean, carefully skirting any mention of our estrangement. Then I began to feel guilty that I'd robbed him of his initial enthusiasm and tried to be more agreeable. When he finally asked about my day, I shared my vision of the slave execution. The moment the words were out of my mouth, I regretted it.

"Poor Maria," he said. "Your visions are such a curse."

My neck muscles tightened. "I view them as enlightening."

"I wish you'd acknowledge the toll your psychic powers take on you—and those close to you."

"Point taken," I said, and tried to return the conversation to the pottery.

But Mathieu had more to say. "Remember Edwina Frost."

Mention of Edwina's name always made my heart thunder. Until I encountered her malicious spirit, I'd always communed easily with departed souls—mostly poets and writers. Edwina's spirit had been such a powerful force that she nearly consumed me.

Mathieu said, "If I had not come home..."

He had been my savior and I was grateful he'd pulled me back from the brink, but he reminded me of his role in the episode too often.

"I'm indebted to you for saving me from Edwina," I said through clenched teeth. "This recent vision came unbidden. It was unspeakable. I didn't tarry at that awful scene."

"If you feel the pull of another psychic experience, promise me you will extract yourself at once. Don't put yourself at peril."

What right did he have to ask promises from me? I hated his patronizing tone.

"Maria," he said, after a moment, "about the matter that caused our...uh...estrangement, I'm sorry I hurt you. Please..."

It was too much.

"I have to go," I said, and ended the call.

* * * * *

That night, I dreamed of the slave execution. I was Constance Creighton, Peter's third wife, and I was sickened by my husband's cruelty. My stepdaughter, whose name I could not remember, was a constant worry. High-spirited, she chafed at her father's rules for young ladies, particularly biblical injunctions to obey, and they fought throughout the dream. In the morning, I awakened slowly, having trouble detaching from the dream. Mathieu had warned to keep away from spirits, but Constance did not seem malicious, as Edwina Frost had been, and I was reluctant to let her go. In fact, I hoped to see her again.

Dressing quickly, I ate breakfast at the cafeteria and hurried to class. The sun felt warm on my skin. I felt attuned to positive vibrations from the universe.

I had assigned odes to the sea. As my Daffodils read their poems, I shook my head at their uninspired images—*raging waves, immortal waters, blue deep*—and determined to show them how metaphors could soar. When we adjourned, I went to the college library in search of Federico García Lorca's poems. There was a master of metaphor!

I was basking in a satisfyingly diverse poetry section, when a stout woman, with a head librarian name tag on her chest, inquired if I was finding what I needed. After I assured her that I was, she smiled and took a chair behind the reference desk. Having found two volumes of Lorca, I retired to an armchair near a sunny window. It was not long until I was completely absorbed in the Andalusian poet's verses.

The elevator dinged. A group of college students got off and spread out through the stacks. One carrot-topped young man was playing rap music on his phone. The head librarian sprang from her desk to tell him to turn it off. When he resisted, she put out her hand.

"Give me the phone," she said.

"Where am I?" the boy demanded. "Nazi Germany?"

"Give the phone to me."

"I will not, you old..."

A girl broke in "Stop it, Billy Ray."

I looked at the girl with interest. She was tall—5'10" or so—and had long ash blonde hair, and wore a navy-blue T-shirt with the words NOT MY DADDY'S GIRL written across her pert bosom.

Why did I think of Constance Creighton? Then I remembered that in my dream, she had a stepdaughter who defied her father. She had not been her daddy's girl either. I looked with renewed interest at the young Valkyrie.

Billy Ray soon claimed my attention—it was the ferocious glare he lashed at the librarian before clicking off his phone and stuffing it in his pocket.

"Very well," huffed the librarian, "You may keep the phone, as long as it's turned off."

Billy Ray and the Valkyrie disappeared into the history section. The librarian walked over to a study carrell, where a red-haired girl was reading.

"Bethia Parks," she hissed, "I hope you'll be good enough to tell your father that Billy Ray was disruptive again."

"Yes, ma'am," said the girl. "I'll be sure to tell him."

The librarian marched back to her desk and spoke to a colleague in a shapeless plaid dress. "The very idea! Implying I'm a Nazi!"

The woman in plaid was behind the checkout desk when I took my books for scanning. Her nametag read *Bathsheba Kincaid.* Two Bathshebas came to mind: Thomas Hardy's Bathsheba Everdene, independent and beautiful, and the biblical one who tempted King David. I handed their twenty-first century namesake my books and library card issued for the retreat. As she ran the books over the scanner, I felt a buzz of recognition. Had Bathsheba Kincaid been my student? A poet from a past retreat? When I left the campus, I realized she resembled the drunken woman whom Bo and I had encountered by the side of the road.

On Main Street, I came upon an old man sitting on the sidewalk with a Folger's coffee can at his side. Bearded and unkempt, he kept his head down. A black pickup stopped. A man in a red baseball cap got out and cursed at the old man, then took off, squealing his tires. The old man muttered, "God damn, Gowdy. Leave a feller alone." I gave him two dollars and passed on.

* * * * *

That evening while there was still light, I returned to the cemetery with Bo. He was in pursuit of the death date of one of the Creighton sons, and started searching in the tier surrounding the mausoleum. I asked where Constance Creighton was buried and he showed me her drawer: *Constance*, read the inscription, *Sweet Flower of Scotland*.

Constance, why did you come to me in a dream?

For several moments, I lingered near her drawer. Did I hear weeping? A sudden gust from the sea rippled the leaves and I wondered if my imagination had carried me afar. I hurried away, in the direction of the colored section.

The sun was slowly setting and long shadows played over the tombstones. The grass had begun to take on dew, and wet the toes of my shoes when I stepped off the dirt path to reach Amen Jones's grave. I smelled the sweet perfume of magnolias.

A feminine voice asked, "Did you know Amen?"

Startled, I looked around. Goddess Jones. I hadn't noticed her sitting on the rusted iron bench. She had spread out a scarf so she wouldn't stain her dress. A youth stood behind her. I recognized him as Lanny Faire, the boy who had refused to pick up Lavinia Dawson's pen.

"I taught poetry at the prison," I said quickly. "Amen was in my class."

"You're a teacher at the Daffodil Writers Retreat."

"Yes."

"You found his grave..."

"I read his obituary and knew he was buried here."

The youth gave me a surly look and moved into the shadows of the trees.

"Amen was my husband," she said.

Now she was a widow. She bowed her head, didn't say the words. She wore a bronze silk wrap-around dress, nearly the same shade as her skin. On her feet were matching pumps. She was either going to or had returned from a social affair.

Or she had dressed up to visit Amen's grave.

"He wrote poems about you," I said, hoping to bring her some solace.

"Amen was always writing poems. He never showed me any that were about me."

"I'd be glad to make copies for you."

She turned her head, as if it pained her. "What did he call the poems?"

"'The Astarte Poems,'" I replied. "Astarte was a goddess worshipped by the Phoenicians."

She murmured something which I failed to catch, so I asked her to repeat it.

"My christened name is Alberta," she said, raising her voice. "Amen called me Goddess when we were little. The name stuck."

I sat down beside her. "With a little work, his poems could be published."

"Will that bring in money?"

"Poets don't make much money."

"I've got two children to feed."

I pitied Goddess Jones, whose beauty far surpassed that of mortal beings. Stuck in this isolated corner of the earth, she had had no opportunity to use her looks for gain. Spooning prunes into little beige bowls at the college cafeteria surely didn't bring in much income.

A retiring sunbeam caressed Goddess's face. She shifted

slightly. "Amen wrote some other stuff," she said. "He left it with Pastor Mungo. He might show it to you. The pastor preaches over on Sims Island. You have to take the ferry to get there."

My interest was piqued.

"He never let me see what he wrote," she went on. "The day he got the message his cousin in Chicago was in trouble, he took all that writing to the pastor and left it with him. Then he went up north."

My mind was whirring. Would Pastor Mungo allow me access to Amen's writings?

"Amen said he'd be back in a week," Goddess added softly.

"What kind of trouble was Amen's cousin in?"

"He was in a gang. Another gang was out to kill him."

"What did Amen hope to do?"

"He knew the leader of the other gang. He thought he could talk him out of it."

The prison guard had told me Amen had killed a man in a liquor store robbery. Had he been forced to prove fealty to a gang lord before carrying out his mission? Had he lied to Goddess about the reason he went to Chicago? Or had the prison guard lied to me?

"Perhaps Pastor Mungo will let me see Amen's writings," I said, watching her face.

"You can ask."

Goddess Jones stood up, cast a sad look at the mound of earth that was her husband's grave, and took her leave. I watched her go, then lingered a few minutes, remembering Amen. When I returned to the Creighton mausoleum, Bo was examining a leaning tombstone with his flashlight.

"I found John," he said. "He died in 1682. Only three years old. William was the only one of Old Peter's sons to reach adulthood."

"Who was his mother?" I asked.

"Emma, the first wife."

We found our way back to the cottages. Before retiring for the night, I re-read Amen's poems. Number Six gave me pause.

Big hipped woman
I saw you laying in a box
A dove sitting on your head
Your breasts peaked like stiff egg whites.

Maybe Goddess Jones wasn't Astarte. She had slim hips. Amen must have seen a picture of the ancient goddess. I sat on my sofa, pondering the life of Amen Hotep Jones. Raised on the barrier islands, he spent his childhood with the beautiful Alberta, whom he renamed Goddess. I wondered at the Kunta Kinte stories he hinted at, but never shared. Perhaps his ancestor had raced with lions and voyaged up the Nile. Had pirates captured him and sold him into slavery? I pictured the long miserable journey to the New World in the cramped hold of a slave ship.

With stories of bold men strong in his mind, Amen grew up in a world that caged his power. So, he wrote. He put his strength into poetry. I could hardly wait to see what he'd left with Pastor Mungo on Sims Island.

CHAPTER SIX

The next day, I challenged my class to compose nature poems with the wildest images they could conceive. We had been reading Lorca and I hoped his example would inspire them. They let their minds fly, comparing loblolly pines to Marilyn Monroe (top heavy), sea grass to Einstein's hair, and the outer barrier islands to a trail of spittle. Proud of their progress, I gave them all a Tootsie Roll Pop.

Afterward, I sought out Phoebe Burns to ask how to get to Sims Island. I was determined to ask Pastor Mungo if I could see the writings Amen Jones had left with him. The ferry, it turned out, ran only on Saturdays. Phoebe said I'd have to pay, but knew a man who would take me to the island in his power boat. She telephoned him. His name was Ian Kincaid, and he agreed to take me to the dock, and then to Sims Island in his boat.

"He drives a blue pickup," said Phoebe.

"Is he related to Bathsheba Kincaid, the librarian?" I asked.

"He's her brother. There are three Kincaids: Judith, Ian, and Bathsheba. The less said about Judith the better. She's an alcoholic—always causing trouble. I don't know how many times Ian's had to drag her out of bars."

Was Judith the drunken woman by the river? "Is she tall and thin with black hair?" I asked.

"That's Judith. Where did you see her?"

"Near the river."

"That's one of her haunts," said Phoebe. "The river and the graveyard. Her fiancé went over the railing into the river. He's buried in the local cemetery."

"How sad."

Phoebe nodded. "She had called him to come get her from choir practice at the high school. He had the accident on the way."

"She blames herself for his death?"

"Probably. Ian took her to several psychiatrists in Norfolk. She always terminated her therapy. I don't know what else he can do. Judge Harp suggested he commit her to an institution. Ian couldn't bear to do it."

We were about to part when a student rushed up.

"Have you heard about President Dawson?" she asked breathlessly. "Her housekeeper found her dead in her bedroom this morning. Doctor said she died of anaphylactic shock."

Phoebe grabbed the girl by the shoulders. "Are you sure? Who told you?"

"It's all over the Student Union. One of the drivers went to pick her up to take her to Clarksburg for a meeting. An ambulance was there. The housekeeper was out on the steps. The driver talked to her."

"Lavinia's allergic to everything," said Phoebe. "Why didn't she use her Epi Pen? She carries one in her purse and keeps another on her bedside table."

My mind flashed back to the welcome dinner. Lavinia Dawson had eaten steak while the rest of us ate crab.

"I wonder who will take her place at the college," murmured Phoebe. "I wonder what they'll do about the Creighton reunion."

Bo Bennett came up the path.

"Lavinia Dawson is dead," Phoebe told him.

"Another Creighton has bit the dust?" Bo asked incredulously.

Phoebe wanted to know what he meant and he told her.

"Lavinia died a natural death," said Phoebe. "The doctor said..."

She looked around for the student to ask her to repeat the doctor's words, but the girl was gone. Wringing her hands, Phoebe hurried off in the direction of the administration building. I invited Bo to go with me to Sims Island, but he declined, saying he needed to visit the historical society library. After he departed, I waited on the curb for Ian Kincaid.

The old man who'd been begging the evening before appeared. He walked with a limp. He passed by, eyes down, muttering. What was his story?

A dark blue pickup turned the corner. I was glad to see there was no gun in the back window. A large, multi-colored dog with droopy ears rode in the cargo bed. The driver braked, leaned over the passenger seat, and pushed open the door. He had the bluest eyes I'd ever seen. The moment I stared into them, my heart sent a message to my brain: Be careful.

Plain and dreary Bathsheba Kincaid could not have such an outrageously handsome brother! I hoped when he spoke, he'd have a squeaky voice and ruin my impression of him. He was my driver, my boatman, nothing else.

"Professor Pell?" he asked in a Nick Nolte rasp. "I'm Ian Kincaid."

Though it may not have been his intent, his voice suggested languid sex under blue skies and pine canopies. Weak-kneed, I climbed into the cab. As I sat down, I noticed he did not wear a wedding ring.

"Maria," I said. "Please call me Maria."

Had I lost my mind? I didn't need to be on a first-name basis with a man I might never see again.

But I knew I would see him again.

He smiled, showing white teeth between sensual lips. Here, indeed, was a descendant of the Cavalier class. Some historians promulgated the Cavalier thesis, in which supporters of King Charles I, through land grants, were the origin of the American southern aristocracy. Ian Kincaid, with his thatch of curly black hair, slightly furrowed brow, and fine nose was the epitome of a Norman nobleman set in the wilds of America.

Lines from "The Highwayman" by Alfred Noyes, sang in my head.

He'd a French cocked-hat on his forehead, a bunch of lace at his chin,
a coat of the claret velvet, and breeches of brown doe-skin.

Ian Kincaid put the truck into gear and headed for the dock. "Phoebe said you wanted to go to Sims Island. Not much to see over there except the ocean. The town covers most of the island."

I murmured a response. I was tongue-tied, giddy. What was happening to me? Falling in love with Mathieu had taken time—at least a year. I'd always been skeptical of love at first sight. Was this love? Or simply a chemical reaction?

We reached the dock, discussed his fee—which I paid in advance—and boarded his motorboat, called *Waterman*. The dog, Sam, jumped down from the truck and climbed on board, curling onto a padded seat. As Ian handed me a lifejacket, his fingers brushed mine. My skin felt singed. Did he mean to touch me? I couldn't tell.

We headed across the Sound. Rounding an island Ian called Frog's Leap, I saw a large houseboat with peeling white paint anchored in a cove. Emblazoned on the side, was the word, *Ark*. People stood on deck, singing "The Old Rugged Cross."

"That's the Sanctified Sect," Ian said. "They go through the islands, holding services. Their members have been doing that since the 1700's. Out on the water at night, hearing them singing, it sounds...heaven-sent, somehow."

"Do they believe the end times are near?" I asked.

"The preacher predicted the world would end two years ago. Now we're living in what he calls, "suspended" times."

Wasn't living in "suspended" times the same as just plain living? Who knew when the end would come? A poem began to form in my mind: *Around a corner, behind a door...*

A few minutes later, we docked. Ian handed me from the boat.

"Thanks so much," I told him. "I'll be back in an hour or so."

"I'll be here. I'm headed for the hardware store to get some supplies."

He smiled. I smiled back, spending a moment too long appreciating his good looks. As I walked toward the center of town, I realized I should have contacted Pastor Mungo in advance of my visit. He might be away. I might have come to Sims Island for nothing.

A clerk in a corner drugstore provided directions to Pastor Mungo's church. I headed up a small hill. The church, painted tangerine, sat like a jewel amid a semi-circle of trees. The scent of pines was pungent. A sign read: Church of the Redeemed. I tried the door. It opened.

Voices. People. I was the only white person in the church and felt uncomfortable. I noticed Lanny Faire. He seared me with a look and turned his back. Behind the pulpit, a rotund man wearing khaki pants and a purple shirt polished a wooden cross. He seemed deeply engrossed in his task and I hesitated to interrupt. Was he praying?

He turned. His face was as round as the moon, his eyes black. "Why hello," he said, "How may I help you?"

"Are you Pastor Mungo?"

He said he was. I identified myself and explained my connection to Amen Jones.

"You taught Amen in prison?"

"He was my star pupil. I've been talking to Goddess Jones. She says he left some of his work with you. Is it poetry? I wonder if I could see it. I might be able to publish it."

Pastor Mungo stepped down onto the floor of the nave, and carefully folded the polishing cloth and placed it on the front pew. "What did Goddess tell you about Amen's writings?"

"Only that they existed and he'd left them with you before going away."

"What Amen left with me isn't for publication."

"Goddess seemed to be worried about her children. I thought Amen's work might bring in income..."

Pastor Mungo took two long steps forward, which placed him close enough that I moved two steps back. "I know all about you," he said. "You're one of those do-good white women taking a black man's words and putting them out for your kind. Amen's work isn't going to be published by you or anybody else."

"I'm, I'm sorry," I stammered. "I didn't mean..."

"Your kind never means anything. Leave black folks alone."

His eyes burned. He stared up at the cross. For the first time, I saw the Christ figure was black with nappy hair. I stumbled out of the church in tears. What did he mean by *putting it out for your kind*? Wasn't it fortunate that people of all races read black writers? Langston Hughes hadn't resisted publication by *The Nation*. Maya Angelou was published through Random House.

Halfway down the hill, I realized showing up unannounced had been a serious affront. My request to see Amen's work was another. Keeping his work safe may have been a sacred trust, made even more so by his death. I had appeared irreverent, carelessly asking him to hand it over. It hurt that he thought me racist. He didn't know that

I shared my hearth with a black man from Africa. And if he had, that would have worsened the situation. I had appropriated an educated, productive black man.

I arrived early at the dock, and until Ian Kincaid returned, sat berating myself for not having been more respectful to Pastor Mungo. The sight of Ian and his dog lifted my spirits. Ian was lugging several packages, which he loaded into the motorboat.

"Sightseeing over?" he asked.

I nodded.

"By the time we get back to Cherapee, it will be six o'clock. I know a place that makes great po'boys."

My experience with Pastor Mungo had taken away my appetite. Still, Ian was asking me to dine with him and I didn't want him to disappear from my life.

I thought of Mathieu and his lover on the dig.

"I'd love to join you for dinner," I said.

Lanny Faire passed by and I asked Ian what he knew about him.

Ian frowned. "Was he rude to you?"

I explained I'd seen him with Goddess Jones in the cemetery.

"Goddess's maiden name is Faire. Lanny is her brother."

That explained their resemblance.

We sped across the Sound, moored at the dock, and walked downtown, stopping in front of a restaurant whose sign showed a pirouetting lobster. Sam, who had followed us, yawned and plopped down on the sidewalk. Entering, we sat at a corner table. The décor was sea grass and dangling cartooned shellfish.

"I always get the oyster po'boy," said Ian.

"So will I."

A waitress in shorts and a skimpy top took our order.

I thought of Lavinia Dawson. If she knew she was allergic to shellfish, why had she eaten it?

"What a shame about Lavinia Dawson," I said.

His eyebrows shot up. "Did something happen to her?"

"Before I left campus, a student came up, saying President Dawson had died."

"Died?"

He seemed shaken. Too late, I realized Lavinia had meant something to him. Once again, I had overstepped the bounds of propriety. I needed to fall into the gentler rhythm of this Carolina town. I thought of the prevalence of guns in pickup trucks. Was it really gentler?

"I'm sorry," I said. "I seem to be making a habit of blundering."

"I was at dinner with Lavinia two nights ago," he said. "What caused...?"

"Anaphylactic shock. Phoebe thought she must've eaten shellfish."

"She was so cautious about what she ate..."

The waitress brought our order. I bit into my sandwich. Ian didn't touch his.

"I can't believe it," he said, shaking his head. "She had so many projects going. We met to discuss some land we own together..."

If I had intended our meal to result in shared intimacies, I was out of luck. Ian Kincaid settled into a blue funk. I ate my sandwich, said goodbye, and began the walk to my cottage. He didn't offer to accompany me. I felt disappointed, for I'd hoped Ian and I would...

What had I hoped?

When I reached my cottage, Bo Bennett was sitting outside his door.

"The police think Lavinia Dawson was murdered," he said. "That makes three."

Distracted by thoughts of Ian, I didn't catch his meaning at first. "Three what?"

"Three Creightons murdered—that I know of."

I gave him my full attention. "Why do they think she was murdered?"

"I told the sheriff about the other Creighton murders and he shared some information with me about Lavinia's death. She had a stuffed pork chop for her last meal. The medical examiner thinks it contained shrimp or crab."

"Thinks? He's not sure?"

"He hasn't performed an autopsy yet."

Bo explained that it was Lavinia Dawson's habit to dine each

Thursday evening at The Seabird, a local restaurant. She always ordered a stuffed pork chop.

"The restaurant staff mixed the stuffing—bread crumbs, apple, sage," he said. "They never used shellfish."

"If the staff didn't add the shellfish, who did?"

Bo shrugged. "The sheriff is looking at who sat nearby. She was eating by herself at her usual table by the front window."

"If there was shellfish in the stuffing, why she couldn't taste it?"

Bo shrugged. "I suppose the sage could have masked the flavor."

I rolled my eyes. The pork chop theory seemed farfetched.

"The other murders were odd, too," said Bo. "Dorothy Creighton was an old lady out in her garden, tending her prize-winning orchids. Someone stabbed her with a pair of gardening shears. Her neighbor, also working in his garden, heard nothing, saw nothing. But as he fled, the killer dropped a red bandana, which he'd used as a handkerchief. There was DNA, but the police couldn't match it up with anyone. Then Monty Dodd, who lived in Atlanta, was shot in his bedroom. His wife was in bed with him. She didn't hear a thing until the shot woke her up. The killer fled. She didn't see his face, but he had a red bandana around his neck."

A red bandana killer. If Lavinia Dawson's killer was the same person, he was certainly inventive—a different killing method each time.

"Do the police suspect anyone of Lavinia's murder?" I asked.

"Not that I know of." Bo stared out at the Sound. "Someone will spill the beans. People have trouble keeping secrets here."

I slid my eyes at Bo, wondering at the veracity of his statement. Environments molded people. The landscape, with its mists, sorrowful oaks and pines, and fathomless sea seemed a perfect setting for secrets.

Telling Bo goodnight, I went inside my cottage and concentrated on a recent class assignment. I'd given the Daffodils a prompt from *The Sighted Singer* by Grossman and Halliday: *Poetry is a principle of power invoked by all of us against our vanishing.*

Grace, a woman with wild red hair, and a penchant for wearing purple T-shirts and bib overalls, had written, in part:

I vanish when I do not speak
When the loon calls and I do not reply
Then I am no more.

More than one class member had showed uncommon depth of understanding of the vanishing concept. Around ten o'clock, I finished critiquing poems, and took a long bath with scented oil. Folding a hand towel, I created a makeshift pillow and rested the back of my head against it. Though I tried not to think of Mathieu, I wondered where he was putting his head tonight. His tent or hers?

A slithering movement on the floor tiles seized my attention. A snake! I cried out, grabbed a towel, and leapt from the tub. My purse lay on the bed. A second snake uncoiled itself from the strap and slid onto the coverlet. Grabbing the broom handle, I stunned the reptile on the bathroom floor. The other eluded me. Frantic, I searched under the bed. Where had it gone? Then I saw it sidewinding into the corner behind a chair with a thatched seat. I brought the broom handle down hard. The snake lay still. Trembling, I sat on the bed. Had someone put snakes in my purse? Were they poisonous? Who had I offended enough to want to kill me?

I remembered Lanny Faire's hateful look.

Grabbing my cell phone, I called Bo. He came at once. The snakes still hadn't moved. I'd killed them both.

"Those are just garden snakes," Bo said. "Must've gotten in when the door was open."

"One crawled out of my purse."

"Here, let me take them outside." He picked up the carcasses and dumped them in the garbage can. After thoroughly inspecting the cottage, I went to bed.

Sleep did not come immediately. I reviewed the day. First, I'd been in the gazebo, then Ian Kincaid's boat, the drugstore on Sim's Island, Pastor Mungo's church, the restaurant with po'boy sandwiches. My handbag had been on my arm or next to me. Perhaps the reptiles had been in the cottage, waiting for me. I didn't think they'd crawled in unaided.

In the middle of the night, I suddenly awoke, remembering the quote from *The Sighted Singer*. Did Constance Creighton vanish because she did not speak? Then I remembered there were traces of Constance. Old Peter had buried her in the Creighton mausoleum. It was her step-daughter who had no name. I fell asleep again.

CHAPTER SEVEN

Morning came too quickly. I woke tangled in my sheet, still thinking of Constance Creighton. Bedroom curtains hung limply—no sign of a breeze. The day promised to be hot and humid. Shaking off thoughts of Constance and her step-daughter, I dressed in shorts and a tank top. When I stepped outside, a soggy veil enveloped me. It was Saturday. No class. I'd made no plans and stood wondering how to begin the day.

Bo was headed up the path in pursuit of breakfast and asked me to join him. He was filled with energy and I hoped he might enliven me through osmosis, so I fell in step. Foregoing the college cafeteria, we looked for an old-fashioned pancake house. Two blocks up, we found our restaurant and ordered peach hotcakes and bacon. The air conditioner was broken. Ceiling fans whirred above our heads. I thought of the film, *Key Largo*. Bogart, in rolled-up sleeves. Bacall, long skirt, cinched waist.

I uncapped the syrup. "What do you know of Constance Creighton, Peter's second wife?"

"Constance Glass was born in 1660 in Edinburgh. Her father bought land in Virginia and moved his family there in 1680. She married Peter in 1684."

"Didn't I hear you say Peter had three sons and a daughter with his first wife?"

"That's right."

"What do you know about the daughter?"

Bo stirred cream into his coffee. "Very little. The only record of her is a mention in the *Annals* that Emma Creighton gave birth to a daughter during a terrible sea storm. Her name isn't given. Why do you ask?"

"Just curious."

"She wasn't alive at the time of Peter's death," he added. "A daughter isn't mentioned in the will."

"She may have been at odds with him."

"Peter disinherited his brother because he was a smuggler, and said so in the will: *To my heathen brother Francis, who has brought shame and dishonor to the family, I leave the scrapings from my boot.*"

What of burning men at the stake? Wasn't that shame and dishonor? I looked out the window, thinking the Creightons were absorbing too much of my thoughts. Then Bo muttered something and I asked him to repeat what he said.

"There are missing pages in the *Annals*," he said. "The same two pages are missing in other copies. There may have been an error in assembling the book for the original printing."

I was about to ask what he thought was on the missing pages when a uniformed man with a badge sat down at the table. He resembled Barney Fife from the Andy Griffith Show.

"Verlie!" Bo said delightedly. "Maria, meet Sheriff Verlie Post."

The waitress poured a cup of coffee for Verlie, and freshened Bo's and mine.

Verlie tore open a packet of sugar. "There's been another murder."

"Another Creighton?" Bo asked, eyes wide.

"Yep. Johnny Parks."

Parks? Where had I heard that name? Then I remembered the red-headed brother and sister in the college library, Billy Ray and Bethia. Billy Ray had accused the librarian of acting like a Nazi.

"Did Johnny Parks have children?" I asked.

Verlie nodded. "Billy Ray and Bethia. The boy's a holy terror."

"How was Johnny Parks related to the Creightons?" asked Bo.

"His mother was a Creighton." Verlie looked hard at Bo. "According to your theory, four members of the Creighton family have been murdered."

"Did you contact the police in St. Petersburg and Atlanta for information on those murders?" asked Bo.

"They're sending reports."

Bo frowned. "How was Parks killed?"

"Somebody caved his head in with a rock. He was in the pasture, watering his horses."

"Who found him?" I asked, hoping it wasn't his children.

"His wife. He was scheduled to have surgery yesterday morning. When he didn't come in from the pasture, she went out to see where he was."

Bo stared at his dessert plate. "Scissors, gun, shellfish, and a rock."

"Perhaps the killer uses whatever weapon is at hand," I offered, then paused. "But the shellfish and gun show forethought."

Bo looked at Post. "Any suspects?"

"Johnny was hotheaded. Had a lot of enemies."

"Any progress on identifying the person who put shellfish in Lavinia Dawson's food?" I asked.

"Did you question the girl who waited on her?" asked Bo.

"Had to let her go," said Verlie. "Motive, maybe, but I can't see her killing anybody. The medical examiner still hasn't performed an autopsy. All we know is that there was shrimp juice on Lavinia Dawson's lips."

"Maybe someone kissed her to death," said Bo.

Verlie Post gave Bo an incredulous look. "I can't imagine Lavinia kissing anybody."

Something came over me. I couldn't breathe. Maybe it was the oppressive heat. Maybe it was the talk of death. I felt trapped in the murderous little southern town. Rising from the table, I made my way outside. A breeze blew in from the ocean, and although slight, relieved my anxiety.

I saw the sign for The Seabird halfway down the block. The bird logo seemed unidentifiable—too slim for an egret, too fat for a gull. Then I realized it was a primitive rendering of a heron. The door to the restaurant opened and closed as two women emerged.

This was where Lavinia Dawson had her last meal. I went inside. The breakfast crowd filled the tables, except for one, near the front window. Someone had placed a framed photograph of Lavinia on the table. Tacky, I thought. Hoping to speak with one of the service people who'd been present the night she died, I hurried to the kitchen.

"Anyone on break?" I asked.

A young man brushed past, balancing a tray of dirty dishes. "Not during breakfast rush."

I exited the restaurant, went around to the alley, and waited until someone came out to smoke. A half-hour later, a young woman with a splattered apron emerged, shook out a cigarette, and lit up.

She gave me an unfriendly look. "What do you want?"

"Were you here the night Lavinia Dawson ate her meal?" I asked.

"Who are you?" She blew a smoke ring.

"I teach at the Daffodils Writers Retreat. I'd just met Lavinia. I'm curious about her death."

"A lot of people are." The girl heaved a sigh. "My friend Judy served her. Stupid cops thought she'd poisoned the food and took her in for questioning. Only let her go yesterday. Judy didn't kill Ms. High-And-Mighty Dawson. They didn't travel in the same circles."

Town and gown. Wasn't there always conflict?

"To begin with," she went on, "Judy had more than one table to serve. She wasn't keeping watch over Lavinia's table." Another smoke ring. "Judy brought her water, took her drink order—glass of Chablis—brought the wine, took her entree order. Stuffed pork chop as usual. Special order, not on the menu. We always made it up a few days before, then froze it. Lavinia's pork chop, we'd call it. I always took it out to thaw on Thursday afternoons."

"Then anyone could have tampered with the meat in the kitchen," I said quickly. "Either when it was made or after it thawed."

"I guess so. The cops suspected Judy because she and Lavinia had a set-to a few months ago. Judy was distracted over a personal problem and ran over Lavinia's dog on her way to work. Lavinia wanted the cops to arrest her and when they didn't, tried to get Judy fired. Lavinia treated that dog like it was her kid."

"Did Lavinia get up any time during the meal?"

"Judy said someone knocked on the window and Lavinia went outside for a minute or two. Other than that, no one saw her leave the table."

"Who knocked on the window?"

The girl shrugged. "It might have been Seth Creighton. He's always looking in windows. She might have left her table to tell him to go away."

I left via the alley and walked down to the docks, hoping to catch sight of Ian. He was there, mooring his boat amid a flock of strutting seagulls. His dog was not with him.

"Maria," he said, "I want to apologize for last night. I was upset, hearing about Lavinia. Can we try again this evening? I know a good barbecue place."

He was in a good mood. I accepted his invitation. We fell into conversation about the heat, the motionless sea. I did not mention Johnny Parks' death, fearing he might not know about it.

But he did know.

"We've had another murder in town," he said.

He went on to say his sister, Bathsheba, nearly married Johnny Parks, but found his hot temper more than she could tolerate.

"Johnny found Bathsheba talking to a neighbor boy near the mailbox and went berserk. Fractured the kid's clavicle. She broke her engagement right after that."

"Sounds like a wise move," I said.

"Johnny had a lot of enemies."

At that moment, the beggar walked up. He approached Ian, asking for money.

"Sure, Seth," Ian said agreeably, reaching in his pocket and handing the old man a five-dollar bill. "Do you know the Methodist Church has free meals on Saturdays?"

The old man mumbled and went on his way.

"Who is that man?" I asked.

"Seth Creighton. He's fallen on hard times since his father died."

"Oh?" I said.

Ian dropped the subject. "Are you doing anything this morning? Want to go out on the Sound?"

I looked into his sea blue eyes and tried to read his mind. Wildly aroused, I fought to keep my response detached.

"Sounds like fun," I said, trying for indifference.

As we climbed into the boat, he motioned me to a life jacket, started the engine, untied the rope, and steered out into deep water. Away from the chatter of gulls, there was no sound but the hum of the motor. The morning sun shone brightly on the water. Away from shore, a cool breeze lifted my hair. He identified vegetation, called my attention to waterfowl. We passed small islets bristling with grass he called sago. Leaning back against the cushion, I listened to his voice—his sandpaper drawl that bought new meaning to words. I was on fire.

"Do you fish?" I asked.

"You might as well ask if I breathe. Everyone fishes here. Women, too."

"And hunt?"

"Look starboard."

I knew boating language. Starboard was to my right. Tearing my eyes away from his face, I saw a rectangular wooden structure covered with dried weeds. Ian brought the boat closer, and I realized it was a platform on which hunters stood to shoot their quarry. I rose from my seat to get a better look just as the boat lurched and fell onto him. He caught me. Desire surged through me like a bolt of lightning.

"Clumsy," I murmured, clutching at his chest.

His grip tightened on my arm as he drew me onto his lap. I pulled off my life jacket, put my arms around him, and we kissed. The kiss was long and full. He pushed at my clothing, and soon I was astride him, as if it were the most natural thing in the world. We both climaxed too soon. I looked around—could anyone see us? We seemed concealed behind the duck blind. He was not finished, for he had begun to lick my neck, and I felt my heat return until I was desperate for him to bring me to orgasm again. He stiffened inside me and I began to move rhythmically. We didn't speak. This time, we lasted longer. I felt sated. He leaned back, closed his eyes. I lay against him, sighed, kissed his neck.

When the trumpet of the Lord shall sound, and time shall be no more...

Singing. An out-of-tune piano.
"That damned *Ark,*" Ian muttered.
The houseboat passed by.

When the saved on earth shall gather on the other shore.
When the roll is called up yonder, I'll be there.

Surreal. An old hymn offering the promise of heaven. The saved gliding by on an ark. Two sinners locked in an embrace.

"We'd better go," said Ian.

I lifted myself, arranged my clothing while he did the same. He started the engine. We headed in the opposite direction of the *Ark,* skimming around the Sound. The old hymn rang in my ears. Like Amen Jones, I had been churched and hearing the singers' words of judgement gave me pause. I did not owe Mathieu fidelity, but I understood when we began living together that I wouldn't betray him. I had just done so.

"Who pilots the *Ark?*" I asked, to distract myself.

"Someone from Clarksburg. The Sanctified Sect has a church there. According to the Sanctifieds, they're all saved, and they come over here to troll for sinners. Some of the island folks go aboard, join in the worship."

He made no reference to our sexual encounter, but pointed out an old oyster bed. Then came the fisheries, the sand fences. He told me about the danger of turbidity, a word I hadn't seen or used in years. I thought it odd that after sharing the most intimate of acts, we did not converse about ourselves. Should he know that I was in a committed relationship until my lover strayed, that I was working toward tenure at the university, that I spent hours thinking of words and how to bend them to my will? What did I want to know about him?

Everything.

I saw an island beyond the barrier and asked its name.

He paused for a split second. "Gull Island," he said tersely. "No one lives there."

"I see horses."

"Sometimes the mustangs swim over there."

I'd read of the wild colonial Spanish mustang herds that wandered the islands. Even from a distance, it was thrilling to see them.

Around noon, we ended our excursion and he returned the *Waterman* to the dock. The pier was crowded with people, taking in the shops. As he helped me from the boat, he held my hand for a moment and said he'd call for me at my cottage at seven. I looked askance.

"Barbecue, remember?"

"Yes, of course," I said.

I did not know what to do after Ian left. Our interlude had shaken me to the core. I hadn't figured out what to do about my relationship with Mathieu. Now I was falling in love with Ian Kincaid.

Tonight, I would see him again.

CHAPTER EIGHT

Most of the afternoon, I cyber-stalked Ian. LinkedIn furnished his resume. He was a marine biologist, working for the state. His BS was from Cherapee College and he had earned a MS in Natural Resources and Environment from the University of Florida. But what about his private life? Online, there was little to go on. I rang Phoebe to see what she knew about him.

"Ian Kincaid? Don't tell me you've fallen for him," she teased, "Most women do, you know."

Phoebe paused for my response.

"He seems interesting," I said, hoping my tone sounded indifferent.

"Cherapee's Byronic hero," she went on. "He's our *man of loneliness and mystery, scarce seen to smile and seldom heard to sigh.*"

I knew Byron's "Childe Harold's Pilgrimage" as well as she. Odd that I appreciated Ian through Noyes, rather than the more randy Byron.

I bit. "What is his great sadness?"

"I don't know that he has any. His work is solitary. He pokes around underwater to make sure the eelgrass is thriving. He analyzes slur—things like that."

"Slur?"

"Algae growth," said Phoebe. "Have you heard there's been another murder?"

She seemed finished with the discussion about Ian. If I pressed her, she would guess I had more than a casual interest in him.

"Yes," I answered, "a man named Johnny Parks."

"That's a murder that makes sense. Johnny Parks had a hellish temper. Few people will mourn his passing."

Someone entered her office and Phoebe hung up, saying she would see me on campus.

* * * * *

The day passed quickly. I remained in the cottage, reviewing materials for the next week's classes. Around five, I bathed and dressed for my evening with Ian. Barbecue sounded casual. I chose a coral sundress and matching shawl with gold fringe.

As I waited for him, I wondered how we would act upon meeting. Was it his habit to take strange women out to his duck blind and have sex? Did he think I was a female Casanova, used to brief affairs? Remembering our lovemaking, I became aroused. Stop it, I told myself, but only half-heartedly. It had been years since I'd engaged in casual sex.

But had it been casual? No. I had a serious crush on him.

Ian knocked on the door a few minutes past seven.

"Ready for barbecue?" he asked, smiling broadly.

Grabbing my hand, he led me to his pick-up. Before I climbed in, he removed a box of vials and put them behind the seat. "Water samples," he explained. He'd been gathering samples to test for morbidity from a place called Cotter's Cove. His conversation was about his work. There were no glances, gestures, words, to indicate I'd given him sexual pleasure only a few hours before. I, on the other hand, felt physically drawn to him. Taking a deep breath, I looked out at the river and counted the herons along the bank.

We drove to a wooded area dotted with log cabins. One, larger than the others, boasted a sign. Barbecue Lou's. Parking beneath a wispy pine, we stepped onto the graveled lot and went inside. A Smokey Robinson tune wafted from the jukebox. Ian and I were the only whites in the restaurant. Recalling my ordeal with Pastor Mungo, I edged closer to Ian.

He shouted across the noisy room to a large sweaty man wearing a sauce-splattered apron. "Hey, Lou! Any end pieces left?"

"Saved some for you," yelled Lou.

"We'll have two of the usual," said Ian.

We sat at a wooden table. A waitress ferried sweetened ice tea and two plates of barbecued beef and pork, French fries, and cabbage slaw. I tried the pork first. The sauce was hot, sweet, and tangy. Delicious.

As Etta James sang the final bars of "My Dearest Darling," Goddess Jones walked in on the arm of Pastor Mungo. Were they dating? She nodded to me. He stared straight ahead until Ian called to him.

"Mr. Kincaid," the pastor said, nodding briefly, and heading for an outside table.

Ian frowned. "I wonder what's eating him?"

"Your choice of dinner companions," I said, describing my encounter with the clergyman, fully owning my mistakes.

"He's touchy," said Ian. "We'll go over to their table after we eat and see if you can make amends."

"I'd appreciate that."

"I knew Amen Jones," said Ian, forking a morsel of beef. "He and Goddess were doing fine until he went up north. They had a little farm west of Cherapee. She had kids from a former relationship and he took to them like a natural daddy. When Amen went to prison, she lost the farm and moved into the Half Moon Apartments across from campus."

"Is Pastor Mungo seeing Goddess?" I asked.

"Is he courting her? It seems so." He craned his neck to look outside. "She's a beautiful woman. Wouldn't be surprised if she was..."

He stopped himself, and then rather lamely commented on a song that was playing on the juke box—BB King's "The Thrill is Gone."

"I saw BB in concert a year or so ago. He's getting old, but the magic is still there."

What had he intended to say?

He was part of the secret world of Cherapee County.

We finished our meal and went outside to say hello to Pastor Mungo and Goddess. The preacher regarded me stiffly, but warmed slightly after Ian explained I'd meant no disrespect when I went to his church.

I hurried to say, "I apologize for not calling before coming."

"She was like my little German Shorthair with a scent in her nose," offered Ian.

Pastor Mungo chortled at the simile, no doubt thinking that Ian had just called me a bitch, and invited us to sit at his table. Ian ordered peach cobbler and ice cream for us all, and we ate the warm-cold dessert with gusto.

"Nobody makes cobbler like Lou's mama," said Pastor Mungo. "She's got a cookbook up at the check-out counter."

"I'll be sure to buy one," I said quickly.

"I suppose we haven't ended the discussion about Amen's work," said the preacher.

"We have if you insist on keeping it," I said.

"There's a book of poems and a parable," said Mungo. "If the parable was published, you'd be pulling scabs off old wounds."

"Then maybe it should be burnt," said Goddess. "Amen wouldn't have wanted folks to be hurt."

"I've thought about that," Mungo replied, "but something keeps me from destroying it."

"What?" asked Goddess.

"The parable has moral implications, and I'm thinking that someday, I might use it in a sermon. I think maybe that's what Amen meant for me to do when he left the piece with me."

"He left it with you," said Ian. "That meant he trusted you to do what's right."

Pastor Mungo stared at Ian. "Knowing what's right is hard to figure out."

They were talking in riddles. I was completely at a loss. It didn't surprise me that Amen had written a parable. He was a poet, and poets live in a symbolic world. He was also, as he termed it, *churched*, as his poems testified: he was no stranger to Judeo-Christian values.

"Amen believed he was his brother's keeper," Goddess said softly. "Look how he dropped everything and went to Chicago to help his cousin."

We all looked at her. Pastor Mungo covered her lovely hand with his chubby paw. A few minutes later, Ian and I excused ourselves and left.

On the way home, Ian said, "If Mungo is going to take a sermon from the parable, it must be about race."

"Maybe he fancies himself another Dr. King," I said.

"Mungo's a good man," Ian said defensively.

Being misunderstood stung.

"I wasn't being critical of him," I said evenly. "Martin Luther King's speeches were rhetorical works of art. I simply meant..."

I didn't finish. I'd never be understood in this southern town. Moving toward the passenger door, I was silent all the way home. When we stopped in front of my cottage, I thanked Ian for the evening, got out of the truck, and went inside.

It wasn't the way I'd thought the evening would end.

My cell phone pinged—Mathieu sending me a photo of Dr. Wachowski's crew. Twelve people stood in two rows. Mathieu was in the back row, near the center. His lady friend was in the front row, left end. I gave her an intent look.

Someone screamed.

I grabbed the fireplace poker and ran outside. A teen-aged girl yelled "Fire," then ran down the street. A woman with a scarf tied babushka-style stood near Bo's door, staring at me. Two doors down, a man rushed out of his cottage in his boxer shorts. Through Bo's window, I saw flames.

My cell was in my hand. I dialed 9-1-1, spoke to the operator, and ran to Bo's door. It was unlocked. I pushed it open, found him sitting motionless in a chair. Fire leapt from the bedroom onto the sitting room curtains.

I shook Bo's shoulders. "Bo! You have to get out of here!"

When he didn't respond. I ran outside. The man in the boxer shorts had disappeared. I called to the woman. She and I lifted Bo from the chair, carried him outside, and laid him on the ground. Kneeling, I breathed into his mouth, pounded his chest. No response. My God, was he dead? Blood ran down his neck, pooled on his shirt. Then I saw his skull was split open. Though I feared it was futile, I sat down and tried to hold his head together with my hands. When I looked up to speak to the woman, she was gone. She had an eagle tattoo on her left wrist and calloused hands. That's all I remembered about her.

Bo was dead. What was the madness in this place?

Firetrucks arrived. Men unspooled hoses. I stayed with Bo's

body until the medical examiner arrived and took it away. Feeling someone standing close, I turned to see Ian Kincaid.

He put his arm around me. "I heard the sirens and came back."

"Bo was my friend," I said.

I wept.

CHAPTER NINE

Ian offered to spend the night. I didn't want to be alone. Bo, Bo, Bo. Memories flooded my mind. Bo as Bonnie in American Lit class. Bo co-founding a campus transgender group. Bo confiding in me, saying how embarrassed he was as a child, forced to wear pink shoes. We had spent so much time together at the Daffodils Writers Retreat. I couldn't fathom he was gone.

Someone had murdered my friend. Was it because he was learning too much about the Creightons?

Ian took off my shoes, then removed his own, and drew a coverlet over us. Shoulders touching, we fell asleep. The ordeal had exhausted me. I slept soundly. In the morning, I awoke with Ian's arm over my stomach. For several minutes, I stayed motionless, waiting for him to wake up.

"Maria," he said softly.

I savored the sound of his voice, saying my name.

Then I remembered Bo was dead. With a sorrowful heart, I stumbled from the bed and spooned coffee into the coffeemaker in the kitchenette. There was leftover coffeecake on the counter. I cut two slices. We ate and drank, and came fully awake.

"Are you thinking of leaving?" Ian asked. "I wouldn't blame you."

"I signed a contract to teach," I said numbly.

"Then you'll stay? I hope you'll stay. Despite what's happened to Lavinia and your friend, Cherapee is a good place."

Was it? It wasn't a time to argue.

"What will you do today?" he asked.

"I don't know. Maybe do some reading for class."

"I promised to take Judith and Bathy to brunch. Want to come?"

I said no. I wanted to be alone.

"Why not?"

"I really need to do some reading. Have to keep ahead of the class."

When he left, I went outside with him. We stared at Bo's scorched cottage for a moment; then I walked over and tested the front door. It wasn't locked and we went inside.

"The sheriff usually locks up," Ian said.

The stench of burned synthetic fabrics choked us. We both had coughing fits. The water-soaked chair where Bo had been sitting was positioned with its back to the door. At the side was a stack of partially burned puzzle books. Had Bo been so absorbed in filling in squares that he hadn't heard his killer enter?

Where was the murder weapon? The poker, in its stand by the fireplace, caught my eye—but its handle was covered with dust. The table lamp bore no blood stains. The killer must have brought the weapon into the cottage. Anger boiled up inside me. Who was this mad man or woman who crept into homes to kill? Bo, Lavinia Dawson, Johnny Parks, an old woman in Florida, a man in Georgia—all connected by blood or interest to the Creighton family.

"The fire started in the bedroom." Ian's voice startled me.

I moved into the bedroom. The wooden bed was charred, as were the dresser and bedside table. Bits of charred paper littered the floor. Ian checked the outlets and said the fire hadn't been electrical. Of course not. The killer started it. After killing Bo, the killer went through his papers and burned them on the bed.

"The killer burned Bo's research," I said. "He was working on a history of the Creightons."

But Bo had stored some of his work in the trunk of his car.

"His car keys," I said.

"I saw them by the kitchen sink."

I collected the keys, hurried to the car, and unlocked the trunk, finding several books checked out from the Cherapee County Historical Society and a thick spiral binder. Remembering the missing *Annals of Cherapee County*, I searched the back of the trunk, thinking Bo might have overlooked it. It wasn't there. I removed the binder.

I'd been talking all the time, telling Ian about Bo's research.

"The *Annals* is missing from the historical society library, as well?" he questioned. "What's in it?"

"County records," I replied, "from the beginning."

"What's that you've taken from the trunk?" he asked.

"Bo's binder. It contains some of his notes."

"Maybe that's what the killer was after."

I tucked it under my arm.

"What are you going to do with it?"

"Find a safe place for it."

"You should give it to the sheriff," he said.

I tightened my grip on the binder. "I want to look through it first. I need a place to put it where it will be safe."

Ian stared at me. "Don't you trust Verlie Post?"

I didn't answer. The truth was I didn't trust Verlie Post or anyone else in Cherapee—maybe not even Ian.

He touched my shoulder. "Why don't you go to the Wells Fargo Bank in Norfolk and rent a safe deposit box?" He stared down at the sidewalk. "Everyone's kin around here. You're right not to trust us."

"I'll rent a car and go to Norfolk tomorrow," I said.

"I can drive you."

"No. I should have rented a car when I first came."

He took the keys from my hand and returned them to Bo's cottage. When he came down the porch steps, he said he was going to pick up his sisters for brunch.

"When can I see you again?" he asked.

I hesitated. Lying in bed, we had seemed closer than when we'd had sex on his boat, but now something was telling me to keep him at arm's length. Waning trust had changed the dynamic.

"Maybe I should come back tonight and help you guard the binder."

"I'll be all right," I said quickly. "No one knows I have it. I want to be alone. I need to grieve for my friend."

His eyes searched my face. "I'll call you tonight. Give me your number so I can put it in my phone."

We exchanged cellphone numbers and he drove away. I took Bo's binder inside and sat down to look through it. There was a pullout ancestral chart, which I skimmed; nearly two hundred individual fact sheets, and pages of notations. Stuffed in a side pocket were newspaper clippings of the murders in St. Petersburg and Atlanta, and Lavinia Dawson's obituary.

Bo's notes were difficult to read and I shed tears of frustration over his undecipherable handwriting. It was "so-Bo," haphazard, hurried. He referred to someone as X, and that intrigued me. Either he did not know the person's name or was reluctant to put it in writing. What had X done? There was evidence of Bo's preoccupation with cryptograms. What did *8fjoria dvd* mean? Or *11wfj Twr*? He also used acrostics to equate X with a tree. Was the killer's surname Pine or Oakes or Maplethorpe? There were lower case x's. Were they the same as capital X's?

The afternoon sun poured in through the French doors. My eyes grew tired and I dozed off. When I woke, it was three o'clock. I turned on the television to get a rehash of the Sunday morning news.

Someone knocked on the door. I peered through the spy hole. Sheriff Verlie Post. I ran to the bedroom and hid the binder under the bed.

"Hello, Sheriff Post," I said, as I opened the door.

"Miz Pell," he said, "I've come to ask you some questions about Bo Bennett. Is this a good time?"

"Yes, of course."

I showed him to the sitting room. He sat down in the easy chair. I took the rocker.

"Tell me what happened last night," he said.

I told him about hearing the girl's scream, then my attempt to revive Bo. "There was a woman standing in the street. She helped me move Bo outside."

He took a notebook from his jacket pocket. "A woman helped you?"

I nodded.

"I don't see that anyone got her name. Do you know who she was?"

"I'd never seen her before."

"What did she look like?"

I strained to remember the woman who had helped me move

Bo. Except for the eagle tattoo on her left wrist, she was a blur.

"Tattoo, left wrist," repeated Verlie. "What color was her hair?"

"She wore a headscarf."

My eyes had been on Bo. The woman had been a pair of hands. Her hands had been calloused, the fingers, thick, nails short.

"I remember her hands. She was used to hard work."

He tried another tack. "Mr. Bennett was working on a history of the Creightons. He and I had conversations about two members of the family that were murdered. Do you know anything about that?"

"You probably know more than I do. There were things he wouldn't talk about, like what was in *The Annals of Cherapee County*. He had a copy, but it went missing. When he tried to check out the historical society's copy, it was gone, too."

Verlie Post stroked his chin. "Reckon we could get a copy from the state library."

Of course. The state library would have a copy. Why hadn't I thought of that? I made a mental note to drive to the state capitol as soon as I could. I wouldn't chance trying to get the *Annals* through interlibrary loan. Ian had warned me not to trust people at the local banks. Libraries might also be risky. People in this small town were interwoven through blood.

"Have you gone into Mr. Bennett's cottage since last night?" asked Post.

"The door was unlocked. Ian Kincaid and I went in this morning. We wanted to see how the fire started."

"Did you figure it out?"

"It must've started on the bed."

"The fire marshal agrees with you. Did you take anything out of the cottage?"

Ian had replaced the keys. "No."

I hoped he wouldn't ask me if I'd taken anything from the car.

"We need to notify Bo's next of kin. Did he have family?"

"His mother," I said. "She lives in Bloomington, Indiana. Her name is Elizabeth Bennett. She teaches at the university."

"I'll contact her."

He thanked me and stood to leave. At the door, he turned. "You and Ian have become pretty friendly..."

It was on the tip of my tongue to ask what business that was of his, but I remembered my plain-spokenness was not welcome in this town.

"We've been going out," I said, keeping resentment out of my tone.

He smiled. "He's a good man, Ian Kincaid."

The sheriff got in his car and drove away. It was nearly five. I went for a walk along the river. I was kneeling, studying the intricacies of a conch shell when distraught voices disrupted the quiet. A group of teens were gathered at a picnic table. I recognized the tall, blonde girl who had worn the T-shirt with NOT MY DADDY'S GIRL on the front. She was agitated. Her friends sought to console her.

"Billy Ray didn't do it!" she cried. "He hated his daddy, but he'd never kill him."

Had the police arrested Billy Ray Parks for Johnny Parks' murder?

"He was in Palm City when it happened. Daddy wants me to go to that bible college over there. Billy Ray went with me to look it over."

"Didn't you tell the sheriff he was with you, Verity?"

"Of course, I did! Bethia told them too. They didn't believe us."

"Didn't anybody see him at the bible college? I mean, he stands out with that red hair."

"Lots of people saw him, but I don't know their names," said Verity. "We just walked around with other kids. Billy Ray wasn't planning on going to college there. He didn't sign in or anything."

I returned to my cottage, thinking about Billy Ray Parks, an unruly teen who defied authority. If he hadn't gotten along with his hot-headed father, he was a logical suspect. But if Johnny Parks' murder was part of a plot to get rid of Creightons, the police had arrested the wrong person. I didn't see the ungainly youth as a serial killer.

Ian called at seven. I assured him I was safe and said I planned to go to Norfolk the next day. Little did I know what the day would bring.

CHAPTER TEN

After class the next morning, I went to a rental agency, chose a blue Mazda reeking of pine disinfectant, and headed to Norfolk, Virginia. Few cars were on the highway. I passed the Creighton plantation ruins and was on a stretch of pavement winding through a pine forest when a lime-green car began tailgating me. I pulled right, thinking the driver wanted to pass. He stayed glued to my tail. I looked uneasily at Bo's binder, lying on the passenger seat—the only reason I could think of that someone would be following me. But who knew I was taking it to Norfolk? Only Ian.

The dynamic changed. The driver nudged my bumper and panic shot through me. Stepping on the gas pedal, I steered back onto the road. My cellphone slid to the floor. The car bumped me again. I accelerated. Pine trees whizzed past. The speedometer read 85, as I rounded a curve. Gripping the steering wheel, I looked in the rearview mirror. The car was gone.

A woman's sweet voice: *The churchyard.*

I looked around wildly. Who had spoken? On my left, a church appeared, surrounded by tall trees. I pulled into the gravel parking lot behind the church, grabbed my cell phone, and pressed in 9-1-1. The green car sped past.

"I need help," I said to the operator, trying to keep my voice calm. "Someone is trying to run me off the road."

"Where are you?" asked the operator.

"Behind a church off Highway 68. The car just went past."

Stay alert. The voice again.

"Who are you?" I cried.

"You're talking to the 9-1-1 operator. Hold on. I've called the police."

Constance Creighton's face appeared outside the windshield. I recognized her from my dream.

The green car whipped into the churchyard, stopped a few yards from where I was parked, and revved the engine.

"He's here!" I cried, and stomped on the accelerator.

Gravel flew as I tore back on the highway. The car slammed my bumper. Speeding toward Norfolk, I listened hard for the siren of a state patrol car. The highway was straight and level. I stomped on the gas, desperate to get away. Keep cool, Maria. I couldn't give in to panic. My life depended on thinking straight. I drove on, the car closing in.

A siren's whine cut through the stillness. As it got louder, I saw my pursuer hit the brakes and skid down a side road. A state police car sped toward me, then slowed. I pulled off the highway and waited for the officer, a petite brunette.

"You the woman who called for help?" she asked.

"Yes. The person pursuing me went down that side road."

She asked for a description of the car, took my name and address, and went off in search of the car.

I took a moment to calm myself. Had Bo's killer been following me? Or was this a case of road rage? Had I been driving too slowly? I always tried to stay five miles above the speed limit. Shaking my head, I got back on the highway and continued on to Norfolk. I turned on the radio. Vladimir Horowitz was playing Chopin. As I listened to the wistful melody, I felt tension ebb from my body. I could see the ocean between trees lining the coast. A thunderhead seemed to be forming in the northeast. I hoped the weather would hold until I returned to Cherapee.

On the outskirts of the city, I pulled into a fast food restaurant for a glass of iced tea. Needing to stretch, I exited the car and sat at a picnic table to type the bank address into my GPS.

Maria.

Constance spoke my name, trilling the "R." I looked up quickly, but no one was nearby except two old men playing checkers at a table.

Maria.

The sound seemed to come from the direction of the Mazda,

which I'd parked near a stand of sea grass. Then Constance Creighton parted the grasses and beckoned to me. She was comprised of pixels—tiny, quivering motes that glistened in the sun.

Her hands were delicately formed. She held a small clock. *I serve to warn you.*

There was a neon quality about her, totally incongruent with a pious lady of the seventeenth century. It was the blink of the pixels combined with the sun's reflection. Her face was sweet; her expression, concerned. I inhaled sharply, held in the grip of communion with a spirit so restless she still walked the earth three hundred years after death.

"It was you who told me about the churchyard," I said. "I'm so grateful."

Did she hear me? I wasn't sure.

There is something...something you must do.

I trembled. "Tell me."

It will become evident, but it will not unfold like lily petals; it will be more like thunder and lightning. It will come all at once. I will stay close. Do you understand?

"Oh, Constance, it all sounds so ominous. I beg you to say more."

A breeze came in from the sea, taking her with it. I stared at the tall grasses where she had stood. From experience and study, I knew that spirit communication was haphazard at best. Constance had done her best. She said she'd stay close. Hopefully, she would say more at another time.

Unlocking the Mazda, I got in and sat for a few moments, wondering what would come to pass, and why Constance Creighton would need to protect me. Thunder and lightning. Was the coming storm real or metaphorical? I shivered, started the car, and pulled onto the highway.

Following GPS directions, I arrived at the Wells Fargo Bank and paid a year's rental fee for a safe deposit box. Before placing Bo's binder inside the box, I lingered in the private stall studying the entries that referred to X. My eyes riveted on *1wg Bonra*. What nonsense! Then I looked more closely. What if the 1 was an L? What if the w was really an m? Then it might read: *Lm g Bonra*. It hit me: *Lime green Bonra? What was a Bonra*. Was it the car that had menaced me?

When had Bo encountered the car. How? When?

I reviewed the newspaper clippings. In Atlanta, a witness had seen a green or blue car in the vicinity the night Matt Dodd was killed.

Notes on the mysterious X appeared on six pages of Bo's notebook. As I read, I realized it was only when he referred to X that his handwriting became undecipherable. Not that his script was easy to read on other pages, but with patience I could make out enough words to get the gist of what he meant.

I made out Lavinia's name (*1vnya*). Immediately after were the letters *Ks o 9th*. *Kiss of the 9th*? The 9 could be an inverted b or d. What if Bo was using numerals to stand for letters? Then it might read *kiss of death*. I remembered seeing a newspaper article entitled "Kiss of Death" in the binder pocket. Rifling through, I found it. A woman in Pittsburg died after making love with a man who'd eaten a lobster meal. Had Bo rejected the pork chop theory and believed Lavinia's death was caused by a death kiss? Was the killer Lavinia's lover?

Then I came across a document that froze my blood: a copy of Avery Creighton's will. He had died recently, in 2013. Avery had set aside his son, Seth, and left his property, which was considerable—9,000 acres—to living descendants of Peter Creighton. Seth Creighton could have a motive: revenge.

Bo had included a page copied from a plat book, marking the perimeters of Avery Creighton's property with a green pen. Using a red marker, Bo had colored in the Kincaid farm, which set inside Seth's family's holdings. I returned to the lined notepaper. In a clear hand, Bo had printed: *Do Kincaids own land they live on?*

If Peter Creighton's descendants owned the Kincaid land, Ian and his sisters might have a motive to eliminate them. Were the Kincaids related to the Creightons? If so, they would receive shares of Avery's property, but lose most of their farm.

I felt bereft. Surely Ian and his sisters were not involved in the murders. I had hoped to explore a relationship with Ian. But if he was killing people...my god...what was I thinking? The Ian I'd begun to know was not a psychopath. He would never have killed Bo.

Before closing the binder, I glanced at a map Bo had drawn, encircling a spot marked "Sunfish Cove," the beach area coveted by a wealthy developer. Frowning, I placed the binder in the safe deposit box and left the bank.

Returning to Cherapee, I watched nervously for the lime green car. I counted seven state police cars on the highway, which was reassuring. Without incident, I drove to the rental car agency and exchanged the Mazda for a sweet-smelling Ford Fusion. Though I could walk nearly every place I needed to go, I wanted a car.

* * * * *

My class met the following day. I put away thoughts of Ian and the Creighton murders, and bent to my books. I'd planned to challenge the class to write a poem on the subject of delight in the style of their favorite poet, but my suggestion was met with a counter proposal. Claire asked if the class could use local historical sites for prompts.

"So many places shriek history," she argued, "like the old brick well house in the park. I heard they drowned a witch there."

The class agreed with Claire, and I changed the assignment. We spent the period working on muscle words—verbs that stretched beyond their original meanings in certain contexts, such as *torque* a primer on witchcraft, *core* a brain like an apple, *drip* words like cider from lips.

I hoped someone would write about the Creighton plantation.

After class, I called the state library to see if it had a copy of *The Annals of Cherapee County* on its shelves. When the librarian learned I was in Cherapee, she told me the Museum of History at Palm City owned three copies. She checked and all were on the shelves. I consulted my GPS. The drive was less than an hour. I pointed the Fusion westward and watched for the lime green car. It did not appear.

Using my Cherapee College library card, I borrowed a copy of the *Annals* for three weeks and could hardly wait to get home to crack its cover. Tobacco fields, apple orchards, farmsteads flew by as I riveted my eyes on the road, careful to drive within the speed limit. When I arrived at my cottage, I locked the door, poured a glass of iced tea, settled at the kitchen table, and opened the book. A poem by Constance Creighton greeted me: "Winter Psalm."

I dip my hand into the winter sea
To feel the pulse of living.
This rig'rous land, which takes all from me,
Has not been gen'rous in giving.

Constance was a poet! Nearly all my spirit experiences had been with poets and writers. As I re-read her words, I felt her pain. She had not taken well to life in a new land. She had come from Scotland, was city-bred, and probably used to an ordered life. Peter Creighton offered her a wilderness of disharmony and strife. I wondered if she had come to the new world with her parents or expressly to marry Peter Creighton. Turning another page, I found a reference to her wedding. She had been seventeen, an orphan, and a distant relative of Peter's first wife, Emma.

Two pages of the book were missing, but as Bo had said, there could have been an error when the document was originally printed. Pages 12 and 13 were gone, but there were no hints on preceding or successive pages as to what the missing pages might have contained. Except for the missing pages, the flow of the book was seamless.

The section on sheriff's records recounted executions at the Creighton plantation, fifty-seven in all, for various crimes and infractions during Peter's and son William's lifetimes. Jacob, William's son must have been more humane, for there were only five hangings while he lived. On the next page, I found a list of the official executioners in alphabetical order: Bigger, Falcon, McVey, Nash, Peterson, Waller, Zane.

The telephone rang. Mathieu. I didn't answer. A few minutes later, it rang again. Elizabeth Bennett's name appeared on the screen. I picked up.

"Maria," she said in a hushed voice, "this is Liz Bennett. I'm at the Cherapee River Inn. Could we meet? I want to talk about what happened to Bo."

"I'll come right away."

"It's nearly dinner time. We could grab a bite to eat at the inn."

I put the *Annals* in my briefcase and took it with me as I went out the door. Remembering a sign pointing to the River Inn, I headed for the highway. As I drove through what must have been a historical section of town, I thought about Bo's mother. I had met her several times when Bo and I were classmates at college. He was considering transitioning from Bonnie to Bo, and Liz visited campus several times, trying to offer support. I hadn't seen her for at least ten years.

The sun was setting, brushing the rooftops with gold. Mature trees cast long shadows on graceful, swooping lawns. It was easy to envision the town centuries ago—ladies in hoop skirts, gentlemen in hunting jackets and high boots. Turning toward the river, I felt a cooling breeze on my face. Then the River Inn appeared, a facsimile of an old plantation house with a pillared front balcony. I parked the car in a magnolia-scented parking lot and went inside.

Liz Bennett, in taupe sheath and sandals, waited in the lobby. Her asymmetrical haircut, though chic, did nothing to liven her ash-white complexion.

She came toward me eagerly. "Maria, my dear. I'm so glad to see you."

When we embraced, I realized how thin she felt. She gripped my hand and pulled me toward the café. We sat in a booth near a lace-curtained window. Lanny Faire was our waiter. If he recognized me, he didn't show it. We ordered. Lanny brought our drinks.

When we were alone, Liz said, "They won't release Bo's body because he's been murdered." She upset her water glass. "So clumsy," she said.

I mopped up the spill with my napkin. Lanny came with more napkins, changed the tablecloth, reset the table, brought another glass of water. Liz apologized profusely to him and to me.

"It's all right," I said. "How could you not be upset?"

She brushed away a lock of gray hair that had tumbled onto the left side of her face. "Bo wanted to be cremated. I suppose I must plan a memorial."

"I'll help you if you like."

She patted my hand. "How kind of you to offer. I think I can handle it. I just need to get his body home."

Lanny Faire brought our food.

I wondered how long the sheriff would keep Bo's body.

Liz cut into her asparagus quiche, then laid the fork on the plate. "Bo had such an unhappy life. The sex reassignment surgery was so hard. What a shame he had to die when he was just finding himself." She looked at me. "The police said you tried to revive him. Did he regain consciousness at all?"

"He was gone when we carried him from the cottage."

"We?"

"A passerby. A woman. She helped me carry Bo from the cottage."

"The police didn't say there was someone else..."

"They didn't get the woman's name. I don't know why. She must have been there when the police came."

I tried again to recall what the woman looked like. Was she white or mulatto? I could remember only her work-hardened hands and the tattoo.

"Bo said he was writing a history of a North Carolina family," said Liz. "Someone was killing off members."

"He was writing about Peter Creighton and his descendants. The Creighton plantation ruins are about a mile from here."

"Do you think someone killed him because of his research?"

"It's possible."

I didn't tell her about Bo's binder. I should have. So far, only Ian and I knew of the binder's existence, and I had placed it out of his reach.

This little town, so uninviting to strangers, was not the best place for Liz to be. I urged her to go home where she had emotional support from family and friends. After we finished, I left the River Inn and drove home. I thought again of the night Bo died and of the nameless woman who helped me carry his body. Why had no one bothered to get her name?

And then I wondered if she had been real? Had she been Constance in another guise?

CHAPTER ELEVEN

Ian was waiting on my doorstep when I got home. I can't say I was glad to see him. Only he had known I was driving to Norfolk two days ago. Had he been involved in the tailgating episode? He may have dropped a careless word to someone. When we went inside, he kissed me. I didn't respond with my usual ardor, and he released me, asking what was wrong.

I sidestepped. "I just came from seeing Bo's mother at the River Inn. How do you console a woman who's lost her son?"

"I'm sorry, Maria."

Throwing my briefcase on the rocking chair, I headed for the bathroom. "What's the matter with this town? I came here for a writers retreat, not to see my friend murdered."

Ian stared at me. "Bo Bennett was gay, wasn't he?"

I stopped mid-stride. "What does his sexual orientation have to do with anything?"

"Nothing, as far as I'm concerned, but there are people around here who think homosexuality goes against scripture."

"Are you suggesting Bo was killed because someone thought he was gay?"

"Stranger things have happened."

"Well, he wasn't gay. He was transsexual."

"I understand the difference, but there are a lot of people here who wouldn't."

When I returned from the bathroom, I said, "Lavinia Dawson and Johnny Parks were also murdered. Did people think they were gay."

"There were rumors about Lavinia."

"And Johnny Parks?"

He hesitated. "Years ago, when he was a kid."

I sat down heavily on the sofa. Was a homophobic killer on the loose? Bo had been so sure the murders in St. Petersburg and Atlanta were committed because the victims had ties to the Creighton family.

"Did you know Dorothy Creighton and Monty Dodd?" I asked.

"Dorothy used to live here," he said. "I only know Dodd as a name on a report of shareholders in the Sunset Cove project. How does he figure in?"

"Bo said he was a Creighton. A year or so ago, he was killed in Atlanta." A fly made its way over the arm of the sofa. I rolled up a newspaper, swatted it. "Was Dorothy gay?"

Ian frowned. "I don't think so. I heard she was stabbed to death."

"Tell me about her."

"She went away to college and became a school teacher. She visited Lavinia now and then. They were first cousins."

Neither of us spoke for several seconds. My mind churned with snatches of remembered conversation with Bo: Dorothy, stabbed in her garden; Monty, shot in his bed; and Lavinia, dead from a spiked pork chop. The only clue was a red bandana.

There may have been more than one killer.

I gave Ian a level look. "Do you know anyone who drives a lime green car?"

"Lime green? Why do you ask?"

I told him about my trip to Norfolk.

"Why didn't you tell me?" he demanded. "You could have been killed!"

His reaction seemed genuine. He hadn't sent someone to scare me off the road. Still, he could have casually mentioned my trip to Norfolk. Loose lips sink ships. The townspeople certainly had loose lips.

"The state police responded quickly," I said. "They were all over the highway when I returned."

Ian glared at me. I'd hurt him by withholding information about the car. He bolted from the chair and left, slamming the door. I moved to the window to watch him drive away.

He hadn't answered when I asked if he knew anyone who drove a lime green car.

Later, as I prepared for bed, I saw a man park a pickup across the street. Ten minutes later, I received a Facebook message from Ian, telling me he'd posted a guard outside my cottage.

The telephone rang. Mathieu. Rain had kept him inside for two days. He and his fellow diggers had assembled in a communal tent for an impromptu chess tournament.

"I miss you, Maria," he said. "I have a terrific idea. Let's go back to Mazatlán before the fall semester begins."

Years ago, we had gone to Mazatlán after pledging our eternal love for each other. We had been so much in love that everything was wonderful, even the sharks that circled our sailboat. Did he hope to rekindle our old magic? It seemed so. I, on the other hand, had little interest in frolicking on golden beaches with a man who'd betrayed me.

"I don't think so," I said coolly. "I'll need to prepare for my classes. I teach three courses next semester. I'm also due to publish another book."

"Haven't you written most of the poems for the book?"

"Most, but not all."

"You might find creative stimulation in Mazatlán."

I didn't reply, nor did I tell him about Bo's murder. I'd begun to lose interest in Mathieu.

"Maria," he said urgently, "I can't bear what's happening to us."

"You should have thought of that before you shagged your girlfriend."

He was silent.

Recalling my interlude with Ian on the boat, I said, "That day, just before you shagged her, were you propelled by an irresistible heat?"

"Maria."

I waited a few moments, then ended the call.

After I turned off the light, I padded to the window to make sure my guard's car was still there. It was. I climbed into bed and lay thinking of the mysteries swirling through the lives of people in Cherapee County. Were the victims murdered to pay for the sins of long-ago Creightons? Were Lavinia Dawson, Dorothy Creighton, Monty Dodd, and Johnny Parks gay? Had they been killed by a homophobic psychopath? Did the killings stem from Avery Creighton's will, which gave land back to surviving heirs? I was convinced that that Ian had killed no one, but sensed he was not sharing secrets, particularly about the green car.

* * * * *

I awoke to the cooing of white-winged doves, so pleasant-sounding that I lay in bed for a few minutes, listening. Reluctantly, I got up, threw on some clothes, and headed down the path to the gazebo. Smiling faces greeted me when I ducked my head inside the door.

"I wrote an ode to the old schoolhouse," said Claire, who had suggested landmarks as themes.

She unfolded a square of yellow foolscap and read her poem, a tribute to a wooden building with a spayed roof and a bell tower ready to tumble. She painted word pictures of a long-skirted schoolmarm and pupils eager to learn of the world outside Cherapee County. Claire was followed by two poets who had been inspired by the old courthouse. Then a young man with a soul patch stood up. His name was Marlin.

"I've written a prose poem about the old Creighton place," he said.

> There's a stump out back where they cut off chicken heads.
> Trees muffle the sound of the birds' final squawks.
> Slaves toil at their work, their screams inward,
> trapped in their bodies. A man writes a will, leaving his cows,
> goats, and slaves to his heirs. Where's the humanity?

"Stark," I said. "You've captured the feel of the plantation."

I listened to my students' poems, pleased they were capturing the soul of the place. Before dismissing class, I urged them to continue using landmarks for inspiration. Cherapee County was soaking into their pores—like the humidity. As I gathered my materials, I noticed a scrap of paper on the floor. It was the beginning of a poem.

Lady Fair, Lady Fair, you cannot dispute
Your bones are gnarled like pine tree roots
Who is your

The rest of the poem was torn off. Who was Lady Fair? Was it Goddess, whose name had been Alberta Faire? How were her bones gnarled like pine tree roots?

I looked up the path. One of my students had surely dropped the paper. Was it Marlin? I could see him at the top of a rise.

"Marlin!" I yelled.

He didn't hear me. I put the scrap in my pocket. I would ask him about it the next time class met.

CHAPTER TWELVE

As I left the gazebo, Phoebe Burns ran up. "Have you heard?" she asked. "The sheriff let the Parks boy go. He verified Billy Ray was with Verity Marshall at the bible college in Palm City."

I'd never thought he was his father's killer. We walked on a few paces, then she said the sheriff had released Bo's body to his mother. Elizabeth Bennett would be relieved.

Once again, I marveled at the quickness with which news traveled in Cherapee County.

"Did they find out what Bo was struck with?" I asked.

"A hammer."

I winced. Poor Bo.

A hammer was a household tool easily come by.

A look of despair washed over Phoebe's face. "This place is getting creepy. I've lived here all my life and though we've had problems from time to time, it was usually with the..."

"With the what?"

"The coloreds." She looked over her shoulder. "Do you think Bo was killed because he found out something awful about the Creightons?"

We had stopped near a live oak whose thick low branches touched the ground, as if weighed down by the sorrow engulfing the town. A black pickup drove by, a shotgun laid across the back window. There was something familiar about the driver—he wore a red baseball cap.

I considered Phoebe's question. "It's public knowledge the family regularly carried out slave executions. What could be worse than that?"

"Don't be so judgmental, Maria," said Phoebe. "It was the times.

A lot of people owned slaves. Those that rebelled posed a danger to society. Examples had to be set."

"If the plantations had been worked by paid laborers, there would have been no need for slavery."

"It was a new world. Where would plantation owners get those laborers?" she demanded.

"There were plenty of hungry people in Europe, eager to get a start in the new world."

I could feel my temper rising. I turned away.

Did Phoebe sense that I'd reached my boiling point? Perhaps. Strangely, perhaps to placate me, she gave up a Cherapee County secret.

"There was a rumor that Peter Creighton's daughter ran away..."

In my dream, Constance had worried about her defiant stepdaughter. "Ran away?"

"With a colored man."

Did the daughter fall in love with a slave? Or was he a freed man? Whichever his status, the price of their relationship was, at the least, expulsion, and at the most extreme, death. A vivid image of the burning man slashed into my mind.

I turned to Phoebe. "What happened to the girl and her lover?"

"He was burned at the stake. Didn't Bo Bennett share any of this with you?"

"He said there was mention in the *Annals* of a daughter born to Old Peter's first wife."

"During a storm."

I nodded.

"That's all you'll find about her in the *Annals,*" said Phoebe. "Old Peter had her removed from history. If the storm hadn't been more important than the birth, there would be no mention of her at all."

"But her story lives on," I pointed out.

Phoebe lowered her eyes. "A cautionary tale against miscegenation."

I felt chilled by Phoebe's story of Peter Creighton's nameless daughter and her lover. Erupting from the haze of clouds, the sun beat down on me, and I was caught momentarily between freezing and burning.

Then as if on cue, choral voices drifted in from the Sound.

"Oh look," said Phoebe. "They've taken the *Ark* out."

We watched as the dilapidated houseboat passed by in the Sound. The chorus sang "Amazing Grace." As the notes hung over the water, I realized the lyrics had been written by an ex-slaver.

A black Buick nosed onto the grassy berm where we stood. June Whitehall, wearing a lavender straw hat, called out to Phoebe, who ran to the car. I walked to my cottage. On the way, I saw Bathsheba and her sister, Judith, arguing on a side street.

"Get in the car," Bathsheba said.

"I won't!" yelled Judith.

"You're in no condition to be running around the streets of Cherapee."

"What's that supposed to mean?"

"You're drunk, Judith. Let me take you home."

Judith threw a beer bottle at her sister's head and ran into the woods. Her aim was off. Good citizen Bathsheba bent to pick up the shards.

I thought of the vignettes I'd seen played out. A black boy refusing to pick up a pen for a white woman. An irate driver verbally abusing an old beggar man. Judith Kincaid letting off steam along a road. A girl named Verity crying over her boyfriend's arrest. Now Bathsheba and Judith fighting by the woods. Squabbles under the pines. Were they indicative of something direr?

* * * * *

Ian came by after dinner. We sat in the back on lawn chairs and watched the sun set over the mainland.

"Did you tell Verlie Post about Bo Bennett's binder?" he asked.

I shook my head.

"It's evidence in a murder investigation."

"I'll give it to him when I'm done with it."

"I ran off at the mouth when I told you locals couldn't be trusted," he said. "Verlie's a good man."

"With no ties to the Creightons?"

"None that I know of." He got up to pace. "I don't like the idea of you being the gateway to the binder. You should give it to Verlie."

I considered what he said. Someone could kidnap me, and under threat of death, marshal me into the bank to retrieve the binder. I doubt I'd be willing to die for a binder.

"Let's go over to Norfolk in the morning and get it," he said.

I didn't have to think long to agree. Ian was right. My distrust began to fall away. He seemed genuinely concerned about my safety. I believed him that he hadn't let slip the information that I was driving to Norfolk with Bo's binder. Perhaps he knew nothing about the green car. After the mosquitos joined us, we went inside. He asked to stay the night and I consented. While I bathed in lilac-scented suds, he sang in the shower. He had a lovely baritone, which surprised me. Afterward, we went to bed, our bodies refreshed and needing each other.

* * * * *

I adjourned class early the next day, and Ian and I drove to Norfolk in his truck. It was raining. The windshield wipers beat a monotonous tune against the windows. Back and forth. Back and forth. I nearly fell asleep. We approached the churchyard where I'd parked to call for help.

"That's where the driver of the green car pulled in while I was talking to the 9-1-1 operator," I said.

He made no comment, calling my attention to a crane standing beneath a church window. We continued on to the city. He turned on the radio. Katy Perry sang about roaring at a tiger. I speculated aloud that her song appealed to people wanting redemption.

"Do you think so?" asked Ian. "Could be she just lived through bad times and the tiger means she found courage."

"Then why is she roaring at it?"

He rubbed his chin. "Got me."

I looked out the window, deciding he wasn't in the mood for a deep discussion about the meaning of modern pop hits. We arrived in Norfolk, retrieved the binder, and drove back to Cherapee. When we stopped at the sheriff's department, a deputy came out of the building, leading a man in handcuffs.

After they passed, Ian said, "What's Gowdy done now?"

"Excuse me?" I said.

"That's Gowdy Smith. He's spent half his life in jail."

We went inside the building. Verlie Post whirled in his chair when we entered his office.

"I saw Gowdy Smith headed over to the jail," said Ian.

"He won't be there long. He and Shirley had a fight. He gave her a black eye. Likely, she won't press charges."

"We're bringing you a binder that belonged to Bo Bennett," said Ian. "He left it at Maria's cottage. She forgot it was there."

Post opened the book, scanned the pages. "Looks like a lot of chicken scratches." He glanced at me. "Can you decipher it?"

"Some of it," I said.

"I may need you to help me."

"I'm glad to help."

Having turned over the binder, Ian took me home and went to collect water samples from a place called Boyer's Creek. I tried to focus on my lesson plan for the next day's class, but couldn't. Amen Jones' Astarte poems lay on a side table and I took them out into the sunshine to read. The first poem compared Astarte's skin to a hound's ear. The second compared her to a song: *I heard the tambourines, the women singing, and knew you were the song.*

Then, the third poem:

> *Your twin appeared in the moonlight*
> *So like you so not. Her utterances*
> *Were the sound of a howling bitch.*
> *Where do you keep your pain on Sundays?*

I puzzled over the words. Was he comparing someone—Goddess?—to Astarte? Whose *utterances were the sound of a howling bitch?* And the unexpected line: *Where do you keep your pain on Sundays?* What did that mean? I re-read the seventh poem:

> *I'll meet you in the swamp*
> *On high ground*
> *Near the Big Cypress*

The one with the howling knees.
Wear a light color
So you'll blend in
With the tea colored water
And foil Bigger the Bear.

What did Bigger the Bear represent? Then I remembered: not what, but who. Bigger was the name of Cherapee County's first public executioner. Where was the water tea-colored? Where was the Big Cypress?

I called Ian. "Where do big cypresses grow?"

"Several places."

"Have you seen tea-colored water?"

"What's this about?"

I told him about Amen's poem.

"Sounds like a made-up place," he said. "Rings no bells."

There was hesitation in his tone. I didn't believe him. Phoebe Burns was a Cherapee County native. I called her.

"There's an island east of the outer banks called Gull Island," she said. "Oversized cypresses grow there. I don't know where there's tea-colored water."

Gull Island. Ian had pointed it out to me, saying it was uninhabited. I had to go there. Ian's *Waterman* wasn't the only boat for hire. I read the poem again and drove to the dock. As I parked, I saw Ian setting out to sea. Where was he headed?

"Someone's set fire to Mungo's church! Burned it to the ground!"

A man in red shorts was running down the street, shouting out the news. He stopped near a storefront and a crowd gathered. I hurried over to listen.

"Early this morning," he said. "I talked to somebody who was passing by on the *Ark*. She saw the flames."

"That's gonna rile up the blacks," said a woman in white jeans.

"I wonder if it was the Klan."

"Was anybody hurt?"

My hand went to my throat, remembering the quaint tangerine church. Sensory images came to me: the fragrant forest smell, the nappy-haired Jesus, the polished pews. A serial killer loose, grave-yard desecrations, and now the Klan? What was happening in Cherapee County?

Backing away from the crowd, I hurried toward the dock. At the end, a blonde wearing cutoffs and a purple halter stood beside a silver motorboat bearing a "For Rent" sign. She was talking on a cellphone. When she saw me, she ended the conversation, and we negotiated rental of a boat named *Mermaid*.

"Don't stay out too long," she warned. "I don't like the look of those clouds in the southeast."

I glanced at the sky. The clouds were ominous, but seemed far away. I knew how to handle a motorboat; I'd done so many times on lakes surrounding the university town I lived in. Ian had taken his boat out. He must have trusted the weather.

"Can you tell me where Gull Island is?" I asked.

"It's the first island after you go through the inlet," replied the woman. "Keep your eye on the sky."

I stowed my purse in the locker, slid into a lifejacket, started the engine, and steered into the Sound. The wheel felt taut in my hands, and then I realized it was me and not the wheel. The weather made me uncertain. Should I have waited for clear skies before trying to find Gull Island? I glided over the water, watching for the inlet the woman had spoken of. A bright spot appeared in the sky. Would the sun break through? Ahead, I saw a moving black dot. It had to be Ian. Where was he going?

Then I saw the inlet and broke through into the Atlantic. God! How vast! As I admired the endless vista of sea and sky, a large wave rolled in from the south, slamming against the boat, causing it to lose speed. The boat lurched violently. I slowed to fifty knots, then twenty-five. A curtain of rain hung in the sky—then it was above me, gushing down, blinding me. A raincoat lay crumpled on the deck. I struggled into it. A strong blast of wind slapped the rain against my face. Lightning crackled. Thunder growled like a hungry beast.

I looked for somewhere to shelter from the storm, but could see no farther than the end of the prow. Surely Gull Island was close by. A shaft of light flashed. Thick black clouds, low and billowing, advanced like a hostile army. I felt terror. The boat pitched crazily and

I fought hard to steer it straight. Then a wave swept me into the ocean. A woman's hand appeared. I reached for it and have no memory of what happened next.

CHAPTER THIRTEEN

What was that pounding noise? Groggy, I regained consciousness on a stretch of sandy beach with the surf rolling onto the shore. Dragging myself away from the water, I took refuge in a tangle of wooden posts—possibly the ruins of a hunting blind. Pines agonized in the wind, their frail trunks bent to the ground. Frantic birds beat their wings, filling the sky. The island had caught the tail of the storm. I pulled off the raincoat and lifejacket, grateful to be on land.

As I became fully aware, thoughts swarmed my brain: the feminine hand, surely Constance's, my own whereabouts, Ian's safety. I was comforted by the knowledge he knew the ocean well and must have found shelter in a cove. As for me, I thought I'd washed up on Gull Island. I couldn't have been far from it when I went overboard.

An uprooted palm rushed by. The wind threatened to dip under my body and flip me into the sky. I felt as if clothing would be ripped from my body. Pressing against the ground, I curled like a feral dog, tucking my head under my arm to protect my eardrums from the wind.

How much time passed? I had no idea, but felt a change in the temperature. It was cooler. I chanced a look at the sky. Beyond the black clouds, the sky was darkening. Evening was falling. Would the wind ever stop?

I fell asleep. When I awakened, the wind had lost its manic force and I thought the storm must have passed. A full moon shone on the pulsing ocean. I stood up. Unsteady, I grabbed at a tree trunk to steady myself. Clouds had vanished, but the moon was bright enough to guide me inland toward the trees. I found a dry place beneath a thick oak, lay down, and went back to sleep.

The sun had not fully risen when I heard a snort and woke to see a mustang eyeing me. I'd read they were unused to humans, so remained still. The horse sauntered off, joining a herd on the beach. A few days earlier, I'd seen mustangs on Gull Island. I felt sure that's where I was.

I was starving. In my purse was a candy bar, but both were probably at the bottom of the ocean. I knew I should follow the horses to the beach where a passing boatman might see me, but wasn't ready to leave the island. I walked deeper into the woods.

Through the trees, I could see the shore, which gave me a bearing of sorts. Canopies were sparse enough to let in daylight. I walked on, looking for a marsh, cypress trees, brackish water—anything that would link me to Amen's poem.

Then I saw it—an amber-glinted pool, its bowl carved from the earth near bald cypresses buttressed with tapered knees. The knees seemed engraved with howling mouths. I was elated! This was the place Amen described in his poem.

Skirting the pool, I climbed to higher ground, finding a clearing. In the semi-dawn light, I gasped. Hundreds of graves met my eyes. I saw no monuments or markers—only crudely constructed wooden crosses. Graves had been dug haphazardly and piled with stones. Despair hung like gloom.What was this place?

I could make out the name carved on the nearest crucifix: Joby. Likely a slave. Planters stripped away proud African names and replaced them with biblical or innocuous names like—Joby. I looked at inscriptions on other crosses. Jeptha, Toney, Jemmy...

A slave burial ground.

The cemetery curved around a massive live oak. I walked slowly to the other side. There I found an elevated grave, bricked up and covered with stones. An iron cross, once painted white, was pounded into the ground. Carved on the side were two words: *Isabella* and *son*.

Isabella did not sound like a slave name. Was she a white woman? If so, why was she buried in a slave graveyard? Was she the only woman buried here? I knelt, searching the crosses for other feminine names. Though I did not cover the entire area, I found five—Dorcas, Ruth, Old Betsy, Patience, and Zasu. Someone had strung a frayed rope from Betsy's marker. Had she been hung?

I hugged my arms, struck by the rising of the wind and the eeriness of my find. Was Peter Creighton's daughter buried in the bricked-up grave? Phoebe had said she'd run away with a black man, who was burned at the stake.

An insect, many-legged, crawled through the stones to the edge of Isabella's grave, lowered itself onto the sodden soil, and mounted a blue object wedged into the earth. Using a stick, I dug it up and found a wide-hipped statue of the goddess Astarte.

Amen Jones's Astarte.

In a vision, I'd witnessed the burning of a male slave. Now, I heard his screams in the shriek of the wind, which I'd shut out as I made my discoveries.

Did the poor burned man lie here? I was certain he did.

Had he been Isabella's lover?

To escape the wind, I moved farther into the woods and sat on a rotting log, straining to remember the words of the Astarte poems. Then, in pixilated form, Amen Jones appeared, not ten feet in front of me.

Pell.

I had a dozen questions I wanted to ask, but remained quiet, except to answer that I'd heard him. He had just stepped into the living world. I didn't know how long he could stay, and didn't want to frighten him away.

Where place this?

His syntax was garbled, but I understood his meaning.

"Gull Island," I said.

But here you.

He was surprised to see me here.

"Your poems led me here."

He stared at me for a long moment, then shouted: *Raise my people! Love them fiercely!*

His pixilated image blazed red, as if he were armored in fire. Moses, I thought. Amen is the burning bush. I covered my eyes against his brightness. When I looked again, he had vanished.

From awe, I prayed to the god of the universe. Then I burned into my brain all that I'd seen and heard on Gull Island. If only Amen Jones had stayed long enough for me to ask questions. Was Isabella

Peter Creighton's daughter? What happened to her? Had her father denied her burial in the Cherapee cemetery? Why had Amen appeared to me? What did he want me to do?

A misted sun broke through the clouds. The wind finally died down. I crawled to the spot where Amen had stood, halfway expecting the earth to be scorched. I needed to re-read his poems, and see the parable he'd left with Pastor Mungo. I needed to read *The Annals of Cherapee County* from beginning to end. I needed to get off the island.

I stared at the choppy sea. No sign of a boat. I thought hard about Amen Hotep Jones' messianic appearance in the clearing. *Raise my people.* Had revolution been his mission on earth?

How much time passed, I had no idea. From the position of the sun, it was probably noon when the *Ark* passed by.

"Hello!" I yelled.

"Sister!" A male voice responded. "We'll send the rowboat over."

A tanned man in khakis and white T-shirt lowered a boat and rowed toward me. The boat slid up on the beach.

He reached for my hand. "Name's Bob. Anybody else here?"

"Not that I know of."

He looked up and down the beach. "You get in and I'll shove off. How'd you end up on Death Island? Nobody ever comes here. This is where the criminals are buried."

"I thought the island was called Gull Island."

"That's the tourist name."

"I was in a boat. The wind swept me overboard."

"You're lucky you didn't drown."

We didn't speak again. When we reached the *Ark*, a pair of hands lifted me on board. A woman named Nellie Mae took me in soft arms and led me to the cabin where she gave me dry clothes—a shapeless dress that hung to my ankles and a pair of cotton underpants. I gratefully put them on, then sat to await her return. She came back with a pair of pink flipflops.

"Reckon you don't wear these things much," she said. "Your toes aren't calloused."

I slipped on the flipflops.

"What were you doing on Death Island?" she asked. "Nobody goes there but the coloreds."

"It was an accident. I was swept overboard."

"We saw a boat bobbing in the water about an hour ago. Name of *Mermaid*."

"That was my boat," I said.

"A coast guard cutter was headed toward it. They probably think you drowned."

"Can you call and say you rescued me?"

"I'll tell Captain Ben," said Nellie Mae. "We're getting ready for a service over in Goose Bay. Can you sing?"

"Sometimes I sing around the house."

Nellie Mae gave me a sharp look. "You don't go to church then."

"I'm afraid not."

"The service will do you good."

I caught a glimpse of the captain when Nellie Mae led me out onto the deck. An older man with a long white beard, he gave me a quick nod. I followed Nellie Mae to the foredeck where a group of worshippers waited.

"This is Maria," she said. "She's going to sing with us."

"Welcome to choir practice," an old man said. "We need to get tuned up."

I knew the songs from my childhood: "Bringing in the Sheaves," "The Old Rugged Cross," "Onward Christian Soldiers." A woman with curly gray hair sat at an out-of-tune piano and struck the first notes of "When the Roll is Called Up Yonder." Nellie May stood in front and waved her arms in time to the music.

The *Ark* chugged toward the barrier islands. I saw no sign of Ian's boat. We sang a few more hymns and then rested our voices, as Nellie Mae advised. We anchored near a thickly forested island and the captain sent Bob out in the rowboat to ferry people waiting on the shore. He made three trips.

Captain Ben doubled as the preacher. He sent up a prayer for sinners that was so filled with fury that I feared he'd have a stroke. "Amen!" we all screamed, frenzied by his fervor. Then he preached a hell-fire and damnation sermon that left me feeling wretched. I sank in sin. There was no way I could measure up. As a teen, I had lied to my mother and stole money from my father's bureau drawer. I didn't improve as I grew up, remembering I'd been impatient with a young clerk in the English Department and made her cry. I'd betrayed Mathieu. All my sins gave me a heavy heart.

Singing the "Doxology" brightened my spirit for it placed me on a plane with the angels, which seemed a safer place to be. Nellie Mae passed a dented collection plate. Coins plinked as they were tossed in. Folks had little to give.

We were anchored next to an island with soaked sea grasses and tall, skinny pines. Branches and debris from buildings floated past. A flock of geese honked and glided onto the island, heading for fresh water.

A coast guard cutter pulled up.

"We're looking for a woman," a guardsman shouted through a megaphone. "Name of Pell. Maria Pell."

"I'm here!" I shouted.

The coast guard transferred me to the cutter.

"We found your purse in the *Mermaid's* locker," said the man, handing it to me.

I waved goodbye to Nellie Mae and Captain Ben. I wasn't sure how everything fit in, but I knew Amen's spirit, the murders, Isabella, the fire at Mungo's church were all knit together. I headed back to Cherapee, knowing what to do next.

CHAPTER FOURTEEN

I needed to talk to Goddess Jones. Though she claimed to know nothing of Amen's poetry, she had to know about his influences—the graveyard on Death Island, for instance. Recalling Ian saying Goddess lived in the Half Moon Apartments near the campus, I planned to see if she was home. The complex was small—only ten or twelve units. I was sure I could find her.

When the cutter reached the dock, I saw the *Mermaid* roped to a post—undamaged, I hoped. The woman from whom I'd rented the boat rushed toward me as I stepped onto the pier.

"Thank god you're okay," she cried. "When they brought the boat back..."

"Was it damaged?" I asked.

"Just a few scratches. Insurance will cover it."

After inspecting the boat, I drove to my cottage, showered, and put on clean clothes. Then I went to the Half Moon Apartments, found the manager's unit, and knocked on the door. A young woman with a blonde ponytail answered. When I inquired where Goddess Jones lived, she eyed me suspiciously and declined to tell me.

In the playground, two children were swinging. A woman wearing an orange sundress sat reading on a bench. I sat down beside her.

"Do you know where Goddess Jones lives?" I asked.

"Why do you want to know?"

"My name is Maria Pell. I taught her husband, Amen. I want to talk to her about his poems."

The woman looked me over. "Just a minute."

Removing her cell phone from her purse, she pressed a button and put it to her ear. "Goddess, there's a woman out here wanting to talk to you. Says her name is Maria Pell."

She listened for a moment, then said, "Okay. I'll send her up." She turned to me. "Unit ten. It's in back."

I hurried to Goddess' apartment and rang the doorbell. She came to the door in slacks, a red and white striped blouse, and a blue apron tied around her waist.

"I've got to be at work in ten minutes," she said, reaching for her purse.

What I wanted to talk about would take longer than ten minutes.

"When do you get off?"

"At eight."

"Can we meet then?"

Her dark eyes were questioning. "What's this about?"

"I went to Death Island and found a white woman's grave. Was she Isabelle Creighton?"

"We don't talk to strangers about Death Island."

It was on my mind to tell her that Amen's spirit had appeared to me, but I held back. A grieving widow does not want to hear that her husband's ghost is communing with another woman. I wasn't sure how serious Goddess's relationship was with Pastor Mungo, but I had taken the mettle of both men and sensed Amen had been her truest love.

"I don't believe in coincidences," I told her. "Amen left his poems with me for a reason. He meant for me to interpret their message. To do that, I need information about people buried on Death Island."

She hesitated. "I don't want anyone to see us together. You never know who reports to the Klan. Can we meet at Amen's grave after I get off work? Around eight?"

I didn't relish meeting her in the graveyard at night, but agreed. We exchanged cell phone numbers. I made a mental note to take a flashlight to the cemetery.

Driving back to my cottage, I saw crews cleaning up after the storm. A tall pine, ripped from the ground, had fallen across a side-street and workers were sawing it into sections. Sheets of colored tin covered a parking lot. In the midst of the disarray, two men pulled a banner across Main Street, announcing the Creighton reunion. My cellphone rang and I pulled to the curb to answer.

Verlie Post. He asked me to come to his office to decipher Bo's notes. "The Creightons are hell-bent to hold that damned reunion," he said. "We need to get these murders solved before it happens. I don't know why Mr. Bennett couldn't have written in plain English."

"He was a puzzle aficionado," I said.

I agreed to meet him at his office and pulled onto a side street to turn around. Entering a driveway, I was about to back onto the street when Mrs. Whitehall stopped her Buick, blocking my way. She had a passenger, a woman whom I was sure I'd seen before. Narrowing my eyes, I studied her face. Then she turned her head so that I could see only her dark hair. Mrs. Whitehall got out of the car and walked over to me.

"Professor Pell," she said, "I heard about your narrow escape. How on earth did you come to be washed up on Gull Island?"

Choosing not to be drawn into a discussion of my recent adventure, I tried to divert her by complimenting her attire—a voluminous teal muumuu stamped with sunflowers.

She looked down at her dress. "Actually, I'm not dressed for the day. I'm dashing out to Starbuck's for a latte." She eyed me keenly. "Mrs. Bell—that's the woman you rented the boat from—said you asked directions to the island. Why on earth did you want to go there?"

How nosey the woman was!

"I wanted to see the gulls' breeding ground."

Her blue eyes snapped. "I've never heard Gull Island described as a breeding ground."

"Doesn't the name infer that?"

She grew tired of our game and backed away, saying she needed to get to Starbucks. "I am not human 'til I get my coffee."

She got in her car and drove away. I sat for a moment, wondering at her omnipresence. Was she the town crier?

I drove to the sheriff's office. Verlie Post ushered me into his office and closed the door. Bo's binder lay on the desk, open to the page where he first mentioned X. I noticed that Bo had written a V beside the X.

"What does the V mean?" I asked.

"That's not a V. It's a check mark. That's where I stopped this morning." He shook his head. "I've spent the past few days looking through Mr. Bennett's binder. Seems like he was pursuing several lines of thought. One was Avery Creighton's will, leaving land to legitimate descendants of Old Peter. He thought the Kincaids didn't own the land they lived on. What he didn't know was that the Kincaids inherited their land from their father, who was from Georgia and no kin to the Creightons. It never was Creighton property."

A weight lifted from my shoulders. That ruled out Ian and his sisters as killers—they had no motive.

"What about these notations?" Verlie pointed to *1w g Bonra* and *8fjoria dvd?*

"The first is lime green something or other." I explained how I'd arrived at that conclusion. "The 1 is an L, the w is an m. The g is really a g. I think this means *lime green*—the color of the car that nearly ran me off the road."

"The day Dorothy Creighton was murdered, a witness reported seeing a green or blue car in the vicinity." Verlie rubbed his chin. "There's a Russian car called a Volga. I think it's spelled B-o-n-r-a in Russian."

"Really? How do you know that?"

"I read a lot of car magazines."

"Who owns a green Volga?" I asked.

"I've got someone looking through state registrations. What about the second notation, *8fgoria dvd?*"

"I couldn't puzzle it out."

"I think I have," he said. "Take a look at these crime scene photos."

I looked. There was a photo of a dead woman with gray hair lying on the floor of what appeared to be a greenhouse. Beside her was a cracked flower pot, dirt spilling out, and a plant with pink flowers.

"I've been studying it," he said. "What if *8fgoria* is *begonia?*'

"Begonia! The *dvd* could be *delivered*. Begonia delivered. The killer could have been a deliveryman." I looked at the sheriff. "How did Bo know about the begonia? He died before the police sent the reports."

"I wondered the same thing and checked with the St. Petersburg police. Mr. Bennett flew down to St. Petersburg and talked with police before he came to Cherapee."

Bo hadn't mentioned his trip to Florida.

"The St. Petersburg police tried to track down the delivery company," Verlie Post continued, "but none had any record of delivering to Dorothy's address. It seemed to them she was targeted."

My mind was ticking. "So the killer gained entrance with the begonia, then attacked Dorothy with her garden shears."

"The housekeeper said the shears didn't belong to Dorothy. The killer must have brought them. No fingerprints. He wore gloves."

I called Verlie's attention to an entry about Lavinia. "Look here. *lvnya Ks o 9th*. I deciphered it to read Lavinia, Kiss of Death. The numeral 9 is probably inverted—that would make it a d."

"I read the article about the woman, allergic to shellfish, who died after kissing her lobster-eating lover," said Verlie. "Lavinia Creighton having a lover is pretty far-fetched."

"Why do you say that?"

"She was persnickety when it came to men."

"What about women?"

Verlie Post reddened. "This isn't like the city. There's not much of that down here."

Fundamentalists believed gay sex was sinful. Poor Verlie couldn't even bear to think about it.

"What did the medical examiner say about Lavinia's death?" I asked.

"Anaphylactic shock. He found shrimp juice in her mouth, undigested bits in her stomach. Her system shut down. She'd taken a couple of sleeping pills and probably had no idea she was having an allergic reaction."

Shrimp in her stomach contents ruled out a lover kissing her to death.

"Do you have any leads on who laced her pork chop with shrimp?" I asked.

He shook his head. "The pork chop was prepared a few days ahead. Nobody will admit to doing it. Seems the kitchen help all had done it one time or another."

"Then it was put in the freezer," I said.

"Yes. The short order cook took it out that Thursday afternoon and left it on the counter to thaw. At least sixteen people passed through the kitchen that day. We've questioned them all."

"Do friends and relatives drop by to talk to the kitchen help?" I asked.

"They do. This is a small town."

I sighed as I sat down in the chair beside his desk. "What do you know about the Atlanta killing? Monty Dodd was shot with his wife right beside him in bed."

"Not exactly." Post scanned the report. "He was shot after she got up to go to the bathroom. She heard two shots, ran back to the bedroom, and found him dead. The killer must've come in through the open French doors, which looked out onto a balcony."

"The bedroom was on the second floor?"

"The killer would have to be fairly athletic to climb up the house to the second floor."

"And Johnny Parks?"

"Parks was out in his horse pasture when someone came up behind him and hit him with a rock. We found the rock. No fingerprints."

"Was Johnny Parks a big man?" I asked.

"He was nearly six feet tall and weighed three hundred pounds. Why do you ask?"

"The killer would need to be tall."

"Not necessarily. We figure Johnny was kneeling, inspecting his fence, when he was struck."

I felt a chill and wished for a sweater. I was surrounded by death and talk of death. I'd come to the coastal area to teach and write poetry, not to be enmeshed in murder. Verlie Post and I fell silent, done with our discussion of Bo's notes. Most of what he'd written we'd been unable to decipher.

"Tell me about Death Island," I said.

"I heard you went there. That's where they buried the slaves."

"Who is Isabella?"

"No one knows."

"Could she be Peter Creighton's daughter? The one born during a sea storm who's not mentioned in his will?"

"Buried in a slave cemetery? I don't think so. I don't place much credence in those old island stories—particularly that one."

"Why not?"

"It's a story told to discourage white girls from being attracted to black boys."

I persisted. "What does the story say happened to his daughter?"

He shrugged. "Old Peter locked her up or something."

Isabella had been buried with a son. "Was there a child in the story?"

"Never heard of one."

I heard a deafening crack of lightning. Thunder rumbled. The electricity went off. Verlie Post cursed as he opened the door to tell his staff to turn on the generator.

The lights came back on.

"Lightning storm," he explained. "Happens every once in a while. It's why we have a generator."

My car windows were open and I dashed through the rain to close them. I decided to go home. Pulling away from the curb, my headlights shone on a drenched Seth Creighton, peering in one of the sheriff's windows. Window-peeper, I thought, and drove home. I found a kerosene lamp in the kitchen and called Goddess.

"It's storming," said Goddess. "We shouldn't talk on the phone. Lightning, you know."

"We can't meet at the cemetery," I said. "Can you come over here?"

"Okay," she said. "I'll be there about eight."

I re-read Amen's poems. If my theory was correct, they were about Old Peter's daughter and her slave lover. The third poem, however, confused me.

Your twin appeared in the moonlight
So like you so not. Her utterances
Were the sound of a howling bitch.
Where do you keep your pain on Sundays?

Who was Isabella's twin?

CHAPTER FIFTEEN

Goddess arrived at my cottage at 8:15 p.m. My heart sank when I saw Pastor Mungo was with her. His influence seemed repressive, and I wanted Goddess to be able to speak freely. He held an umbrella to cover her. It was dripping. I took it to the bathroom to drain into the tub.

Returning, I said, "I'm so sorry your church burned down, Pastor Mungo. Does the sheriff know who was responsible?"

"Men in white robes."

"Cowards," said Goddess. "They cover their faces."

"If there's a klavern around here, the sheriff must know who the members are," I said.

"Don't talk to me about that sheriff," said the pastor. "Why did you want to see Goddess?"

"Please sit down," I said. "Would you like something to drink?"

They sat on the sofa. Goddess asked for water. Pastor Mungo shook his head.

When I returned from the kitchen with Goddess' glass of ice water, I said, "I want to talk about Isabella."

The pastor looked at me coldly. "We don't discuss people buried on Death Island. It riles folks."

"That's what you said about Amen's parable. Are Death Island and the parable connected?"

He didn't answer.

"Do you still have the parable?" I asked. Hopefully, it hadn't been destroyed in the fire.

"It's safe. I keep it at the parsonage."

Goddess broke in. "Why are you so interested in our past?"

It was a fair question.

"Because Amen wrote about it in his poems. I want to know more to better understand what he wrote."

If Goddess had come alone, I might have confessed that I'd communed with Amen's spirit, but she had brought Pastor Mungo, who was sure to have a dim view of the supernatural.

"Why do you want to know about Isabella?" asked Goddess.

"I think Isabella is the Astarte of his poems. I found a statue of Astarte at her grave."

"Amen placed it there," said Goddess.

"Don't say any more," cautioned Pastor Mungo.

I turned to him. "There's another reason I'm interested in Cherapee County's past. Bo Bennett was my friend. Someone murdered him because he was researching the Creighton murders. I want to know who killed Bo."

"You put yourself in peril, trying to find that out," said Pastor Mungo.

"You're a man of God," I protested. "You should care about what's happening here."

"What white people do to each other is not my concern," he said.

"Oh, Charles," said Goddess, "you know that's wrong. Tell Maria about Amen's parable."

"Publicizing the parable will cause more deaths," said Mungo.

I could tell by the set of his jaw that the pastor would not easily share the parable. Even Goddess's appeals failed to move him. I looked away, not knowing what to say.

Then Goddess said, "I can't tell you about Amen's parable because I've never read it, but I can tell you about Isabella and Drake."

"No!" said the pastor.

"Who is Drake?" I asked.

"Drake isn't a secret, Charles. Most people know about him."

"She isn't one of us."

"We're all members of the human race," Goddess shot back. "That's what Amen used to say."

"Amen, Amen," Pastor Mungo said exasperatedly. "You talk about him as if he was a...a...saint."

Goddess narrowed her eyes. "How do you know he wasn't?"

They both fell silent. So did I.

Then Pastor Mungo leapt up and began pacing the cramped dimensions of my sitting room, causing the floors to creak. After he nearly knocked a lamp off an end table, he stopped to scowl at me.

"I'll show you what Amen left with me, Professor Pell," he said, "but you may not publish it."

"All right," I said. I would have agreed to see the parable under any terms.

I arranged to go to the parsonage the following day, and Goddess and the pastor left. It was only when I saw their headlights turn on that I remembered Isabella and Drake. Goddess had not told their story.

I took the kerosene lamp into my bedroom and undressed. Before lying down, I looked out the window to see if my guard's car was parked on the street. It had begun to rain again. Without streetlights, darkness consumed the night. I couldn't tell if the guard was there.

After checking locks on my windows and doors, I turned out the lamp and went to bed. Unable, to sleep, I kept thinking of Isabella. She had to be Old Peter's daughter. Did she have children other than the son she was buried with?

It was fortunate I was awake.

Someone was tinkering with the lock on the French doors. For an instant, I froze. Then, realizing I was the only one who could ensure my safety, I threw on my robe, grabbed the fireplace poker, slipped out the front door, and crept to the rear of the cottage. A figure knelt in front of the French doors, a flashlight held in his teeth. Metal scraped as he picked the lock. He slid open the door, stepped into the cottage. Through the bedroom window, I saw a speck of light dart like a firefly, then hover above my bed.

Two gunshots—one—two—shattered the night.

The intruder had shot my duvet, thinking I was under it.

I gasped. Should I run? Fury burned inside me. What had I done in this hateful town to cause someone to want to murder me? Moving closer to the doors, I hefted the poker and waited. He came out. I struck hard, missing his head, but hitting his shoulder. He cried out. A woman's voice! She fell to the ground.

As I braced myself to strike a second blow, she got up and ran. I stared into the darkness, and then stepped inside the cottage. My bare foot hit something hard—the gun. I picked it up and leaned against the wall, trying to calm myself.

The lights flickered on.

"Maria!"

Ian's voice. He was beating on the front door. I dropped the gun into my robe pocket, and ran to let him in. I felt his arms around me. His dogs mobbed our legs, then tore into the cottage, barking furiously.

"Are you all right?" Ian's breath was warm against my neck. "I was taking over guard duty and heard the shot."

"A woman tried to kill me."

I felt his muscles tighten. "Did you see where she went?"

"It was too dark.

He released me. "Was anything familiar about her?"

I thought for a moment. "No. I think she was about my height. I got the impression she had an athletic build."

"Have you ever seen my sister Judith?"

"A couple of times. She's thinner than this woman. Why would your sister want to kill me?"

"Who knows what goes on in her head? She's drunk all the time. Lately, she's taken to shooting seagulls in the orchard because they mess on the fruit. I tried to take the gun away, but she hid it."

"Surely the person who shot at me is the same person who killed Bo—and maybe the Creightons. Judith can't be a serial killer." I remembered the gun in my pocket. "Here's the shooter's gun. Is it Judith's?"

He took the gun and examined it. "This is a Smith & Wesson .38 special. That's what Judith's is." He stared at me. "Get some clothes on. I can't leave you here alone with someone trying to kill you. I'm going to the farm to see if Judith's there. I have to find out if she's been shooting at people."

My head was spinning. "Why would Judith want to kill me?"

"Maybe she resents you. She and Bathy are afraid I'll bring a woman to live in the house."

Two old maids, living out their lives in the ancestral home, fearing their brother would bring a wife into the house, and disturb their cradle-to-the-grave existence.

I was incredulous. "And for that, she's willing to kill me?"

Ian didn't answer. As I threw on jeans and a T-shirt, I considered the plight of the Kincaid sisters. Judith apparently gave up on life when her lover died, but Bathsheba worked at the library. Had she gone away to college? Or did Cherapee College offer a library science degree? I joined Ian outside. He whistled for his dogs and they jumped into the back of the truck.

"I left a message on Verlie's answering machine that someone tried to kill you," he said, as we climbed in the truck. "I told him I was taking you to the farm."

"Did you mention Judith?"

"I said she might have been the shooter."

We sped through the watery streets of Cherapee, then drove along the coast on a winding, single-track-road with grass growing down the middle. Though the rain had stopped, lighting still forked the sky. I felt drained. Was the attempt on my life connected to the Creighton murders?

"I heard you went to Gull Island," Ian said.

"Death Island."

"White people call it Gull Island," he said. "It's no place for you to go, Maria. You shouldn't have taken a boat out. The weather was too threatening."

"You were out on the Sound."

"I know these waters. I was trying to find Judith. There was some trouble at one of the bars and the manager called me. One of the guys at the bar had taken her out in his boat."

"How old is Judith?" I asked.

"Thirty-six."

Headlights approached. Ian moved to the right side of the road to allow room for a county car.

"That's Verlie," said Ian.

The car stopped. Verlie Post rolled down his window. "That you, Ian? There's been a bit of trouble at your house. Someone was prowling around the house and scared Bathsheba. Deputy Guidry is there."

"This has been a busy night for prowlers," said Ian. "I left a message on your answering machine. Someone broke into Maria's cottage and shot at the bed, thinking she was in it. Whoever it was dropped the gun. It might have been Judith."

"Give it here," said Verlie. "I gathered from Bathsheba that Judith was missing. Do you know where she is?"

Ian gave the gun to the sheriff. "Your guess is as good as mine. She'll come home. When she does, I'll bring her in."

The sheriff went on his way, leaving an attempted murderer at large. I shook my head at the slackness with which laws were enforced in the county. No wonder Verlie Post had made little progress in solving the Creighton murders.

Ian put the truck in gear and stepped on the accelerator. When we reached the Kincaid property, two pole lights projected a twinkling radiance onto the landscape. Buildings—barn, crib, possibly a toolshed—seemed to loom, their upper structures graced with light, the lower levels, dark and brooding. Ian parked next to a wrought-iron gate decorated with cherubs. The domicile appeared to be a restored pre-Civil War mansion. We went up steps leading to a wide verandah. Ian held open a large door with a stained-glass window. The entry, which extended into a hall, was hung with portraits; Cavalier types with ruffles at their throats, ladies in modest décolletage.

"The Kincaids are also part of the old aristocracy," I said.

"Not the Kincaids," he said. "The Fraziers, through my mother's side."

We came to a large door, painted emerald green. Ian pulled it open. Steps led to a cellar kitchen. Deputy Guidry sat at a long trencherman's table. Bathsheba, her hair unkempt, sat beside him. Another woman, who turned out to be a neighbor named Maddy, poured coffee into mugs.

When Bathsheba saw her brother, she jumped up. "Oh, Ian. I'm so glad you're home. Somebody was trying to get inside the house. I made sure all the doors and windows were locked. I was so scared, I pushed furniture up against the doors."

"Did you see who it was?"

"No. No, I didn't." Bathsheba wrung her hands. "I called Maddy to come over. It would have to happen when Judith..."

"Do you know where Judith is?" demanded Ian.

"I was just about to say she was gone."

The green door swung open. Judith Kincaid stood there, looking like a drowned rat. She paused in the entryway to remove muddy shoes.

Bathsheba ran to her. "Someone tried to get in the house, Judith. I was so scared I called the sheriff."

"You're such a fraidy-cat, Bathy. That was me. The fog was so thick I couldn't find the door."

Judith Kincaid swept the room with nervous eyes. What did she think when she saw me? Had she tried to kill me an hour earlier?

She rubbed her shoulder. "I need a cold compress, Bathy," she said in a little girl voice. "I fell and hurt my arm."

I tensed. Was she suffering from a blow from my poker?

"Maddy, can you get the ice bag?" asked Bathsheba. "It's in the wash room cabinet."

"Where have you been, Judith?" asked Ian.

"Just out for a ride in the rain." Judith took a step forward, lost her balance, and steadied herself with a hand on the wall. "I need to get out of these wet clothes."

She lurched toward the staircase with Ian following. They returned several minutes later. Bathsheba had changed into a faded blue chenille robe and slippers.

"Well, I see someone's made coffee," she said, a smile curving her lips. "There's banana nut bread in the breadbox. Would y'all like some?" She sat down. "Bathy, you should get the plates. I can't work my arm very well."

Maddy brought the ice bag, draped it over Judith's shoulder. As Bathsheba opened the cupboard to take down the plates, Ian whispered in my ear that it wasn't Judith who tried to shoot me. She'd been climbing stiles in a soggy meadow with her drunken pal Lester. He'd called Lester for verification, and then notified the sheriff that it had not been Judith who broke into my cottage.

Then who had?

Bathsheba retrieved the nut bread from the breadbox and placed it on a pewter plate. I could not help but notice the quick precision with which she moved. Poised above a wooden block, her hands selected a knife, sliced the bread, and slid it onto the plates.

Maddy brought forks to the table.

My eyes roved around the beamed, low-ceilinged room. I guessed it to be the original kitchen, remodeled over the centuries. Against the wall was a stone fireplace with a hearth extending six feet into the room. Two wooden benches, cushioned and laid with faded quilts, flanked the hearth. The cupboards had been replaced, but the hinges looked old. Brass, I thought. Cabinet tops were decorated with plaster animals—a rooster, two bears, an oversized squirrel.

A vision came, and with it, the smell of ham roasting on the spit. I heard low-pitched voices, the clink of a metal spoon against crockery, the slam of a door as someone brought in peaches from the orchard. *Don't slam that door, boy!* said an irate old woman, sitting on a stool, snapping beans.

The kitchen was filled with slaves stoking the fire, brewing tea in an iron pot hanging over the flames, sweeping the floor with a straw broom. The cook floured pieces of cut-up chicken and placed them in a skillet of bubbling lard. I remembered the tenth Astarte poem:

> *The duck's in the pan*
> *The coals are hot;*
> *Its screams are heard*
> *Throughout the land.*

Drake was the duck.

Suddenly Amen Jones's spirit burst from a wall, his luminosity lighting up the room. The slaves stopped what they were doing to stare at him and fell to their knees. He carried a cartouche, a scroll-like tablet, which he turned to us so we could read what was written. It was a message—a message for me. Though, I strained my eyes, I could not read the words.

"What?" I asked. "What do you want of me?"

Did he speak the word *parable*? I thought he did. He vanished, taking the vision with him.

"What's that you said?" asked Bathsheba.

I turned to her. "I was thinking aloud. Mumbling. Sorry."

She looked at me strangely and passed the plates of nut bread. I took one, but had no appetite. Deputy Guidry ate his portion, so did the women. Ian fussed with his.

I was still reeling from Amen's appearance. His spirit had grown quite bold.

"Ian," said Judith, "Your Yankee lady friend hasn't touched her goody."

"I'm sure it's delicious," I said, "but I'm not hungry this late at night."

"But you are for my brother," she said, raising one eyebrow.

I blushed furiously.

"Ian," I said stiffly, "please take me home."

"Yes, it's time," he said.

We rode back to my cottage in silence. There was enough to trouble my mind without discussing his sisters' weirdness. He came inside and locked the door. I spent what remained of the night in his arms and slept, feeling safe.

CHAPTER SIXTEEN

On Saturday, the sheriff came to the cottage to examine scratches on the lock and the bullet hole in my pillow.

"Why would anyone want to kill you?" asked Verlie Post.

"My guess is my association with Bo Bennett," I said.

"Maria's been going around asking questions," said Ian.

I looked at him sharply.

"You questioned the sous chef at The Seabird," he said. "You've been talking to Pastor Mungo and Goddess Jones."

"You need to stop, Miz Pell." Verlie Post said sternly. "Let the law do the asking."

"Have you been following me around, Ian?" I demanded.

"You know I haven't. People gossip when a stranger goes around asking questions."

Not trusting myself to speak, I strode over to my kitchen window. Seth Creighton peered in at me. I screamed.

"That's just old Seth," said the sheriff. "He's always peeking in windows. I'll go shoo him away."

He went outside. I looked askance at Ian. He shrugged, shook his head.

When Verlie returned, he said, "The Creighton reunion is in three days. They're putting up the tents. I've assigned six men to the park."

"Good idea," said Ian.

The men discussed the best way to safeguard the Creightons and I tuned them out, focusing on Amen and his cartouche. *Parable.* I was sure he said *parable.* I had to read it.

After the sheriff left, I asked Ian to take me to Sims Island, telling him that Pastor Munro had agreed to let me see Amen Jones' parable.

"Why can't you let this stuff go?" he demanded. "Just be a poet, teach your class, and stay out of things that aren't any of your business."

I wanted to say: Bo Bennett was murdered, and at the rate your sheriff is solving the crime, the killer will never be found.

Instead, I said, "Ian, let's not argue over this. I came here, wanting to find out more about Amen Jones' poems. Now that I know he left a parable, I want to see it. I may be able to get his work published. That would mean a source of income for Goddess and her children."

He mulled it over. "All right, I'll take you to Sims Island."

On the way to the dock, he stopped to check on storm damage to Sunfish Cove. A pine had fallen, blocking the road to the beach. He got out of the truck, examined the tree, and called someone to haul it away.

Despite the downed tree and debris, the cove had survived the storm well. The sun picked up sparkling bits of mica in the sand and the ocean front was gleeful as it struck the beach. Idyllic, I thought. A coastal treasure.

"This is a beautiful property," I remarked, when Ian returned to the truck.

"We hope to turn it into a public park so everyone can enjoy it," he said.

"I heard a billionaire wanted to buy it and turn it into a resort."

He grunted something unintelligible and started the truck.

* * * * *

Around one o'clock, we left for the island. The sun was bright, and aside from a few floating branches, the Sound was clear of detritus from the storm. Would Pastor Mungo welcome Ian since he had not invited him? I hoped Ian would find something else to do.

As it turned out, a man in an orange cap detained him at the pier, asking about the water quality near his cove, and I went up the hill alone to the parsonage. The sight of the burned-out church, now a husk, staggered me. The walls still stood, but the roof had caved in.

I thought of the pews, the crucifix, the pulpit, all so lovingly cared for by the pastor and his congregation. Whoever set fire to the church struck at the very foundation of black culture in Cherapee County. White sheets, Reverend Mungo had said. Race hatred sickened me.

Pastor Mungo stood in his yard, surveying the site.

"Will insurance cover the damage?" I asked, as I approached.

"The church was built thirty years ago. Building costs have skyrocketed since then. We'll have to rebuild slowly as we raise funds."

A woman in a jeep pulled up in front of the church. She looked familiar. I thought I'd seen her with June Whitehall.

"Let's go inside" said Pastor Mungo. "I don't want to talk to that woman. She's with some organization Mrs. Whitehall heads. They want to buy the church property."

"What organization?"

"I don't know what it's called," he answered. "It meets in the park rotunda. I think it has to do with historical preservation."

I cast a look at the woman before I went into the parsonage. Her straw hat was tipped so I couldn't see her face. Glancing downhill, I saw Ian still engaged in conversation with the orange-capped man.

Inside the parsonage, Pastor Mungo asked me to sit down while he went upstairs to get the parable. I heard drawers scraping, doors banging. Had he misplaced it? He came downstairs, a distraught look on his face.

"Someone's taken it and all of Amen's research. It must have happened during the fire. People were all over the place. It would have been a simple thing to come into the house..."

I envisioned the pandemonium—firetrucks, people trying to help, children getting in the way.

"Who knew of the parable's existence?" I asked.

"Goddess, her brother Lanny, you, Ian Kincaid," said the pastor. "Did Bo Bennett know about it?"

I thought for a moment. "He knew Amen had written something and left it with you."

Ian knocked on the door. Pastor Mungo admitted him.

"Someone's stolen the parable," I said.

Pastor Mungo explained that he had kept it in his study. He last looked at it the day before the fire and was sure he'd replaced it in the desk drawer.

"What was the parable about?" asked Ian.

"Racial unity," said the pastor.

"There's nothing new in that," said Ian.

"Amen showed how everyone was related."

"Sure," replied Ian. "We're all part of the human race."

"No," the pastor said patiently, "really related."

I sucked in my breath, straining to recall the lineage chart in Bo's notebook.

Ian's eyes widened. "What do you mean?"

Pastor Mungo left the room.

"Color lines were blended," I said softly. "I'll bet that's what the parable is about."

"Words," Ian said, crossly. "Myths. Unsubstantiated theories."

I glanced at him sharply, thinking of Thomas Paine's *Common Sense* and Harriet Beecher Stowe's *Uncle Tom's Cabin*. Words could set the world on fire. Didn't he know that?

Ian sat down heavily on the sofa and stared at the floor. I sensed he was struggling to extricate himself from layers of racism. I didn't know how to help him. After a moment, I said we should leave.

We found Pastor Mungo in his study, said goodbye, and left. We were quiet as we skimmed back across the Sound. More than a cool breeze separated us.

On reaching shore, we climbed in Ian's pickup and drove through town. At the riverside park, a banner strung between two trees heralded the three hundredth anniversary of the Creighton re-union. People had come together for three hundred years to celebrate family! Wind whipped the tents, billowing them like sails on a schooner. Park employees had placed a dais on a grassy berm, then arranged twelve long picnic tables like spokes in a semi-circle. June Whitehall circulated among the workers, giving orders.

"Pastor Mungo said June represents an organization interested in purchasing his church's property," I said.

"June is an organization in herself," Ian said shortly. "She has her fingers in every pie."

"Is she interested in preserving county heritage?"

"You could say that," he said. "Look at the water in that pond. It's kind of a sickly shade of green. I need to grab a bottle and get a specimen."

The water looked fine to me, but what did I know? I wrote poetry. Ian swerved into the park, drove to the pond, and got out to take a water sample. June noticed him and hurried to see what he was up to.

"Is that water bad?" she demanded.

"I'm going to analyze it and see."

"I hope you do it quickly. I would have thought you would have already sampled the water. After all, the reunion is an important event. The hotels and B&B's are all filled up."

"I have to send the sample to Raleigh," he said unapologetically.

She shook her head and headed back to the dais.

Ian returned to the truck. "Uppity woman," he muttered. "Just because she's descended from Old Peter's son, she thinks she runs everything."

I became alert. "As opposed to..."

"Mungo's right. There are Creightons with black blood."

"Peter had a slave mistress?"

Ian didn't answer. He put the truck in gear and drove back into the street, passing a truck loaded with portable toilets destined for the park. When I got home, I tried to put thoughts of the Creightons out of my mind and prepare for the next day's class. Ian needed to test the water at Salt Creek and do some paperwork, but asked to come back to spend the night.

I agreed. After he left, I sat down to plan Monday's class. I'd meant to talk about Robert Frost, but as I flipped through an anthology, I came across a poem by Gjertrud Schnackenberg, who used rhyme and meter ingeniously. Perhaps we'd explore some of her work. I tried to amend my lesson plan, but Cherapee County and its secrets invaded my thoughts. I closed my eyes, inhaled deeply several times, and bid Constance Creighton to come to me. Though I sat in a semi-trance for several minutes, I was unable to reach her. Just as I was about to give up, I heard a breathless voice—perhaps Amen's—say *Astarte*.

Yes! The Astarte poems!

I'd save Schnackenberg for another time. I decided to make copies of Amen's poems for the class and see what they made of them. Since they had been absorbing the history of the area, maybe they could help me unlock Cherapee's secrets.

Ian returned in time for supper. I fixed BLTs, and we sat outside to eat.

"I'm sorry for everything," he said.

I opened my mouth to ask what he meant, but one glance at his face, darkened with worry, silenced me.

CHAPTER SEVENTEEN

The morning broke with sunshine, a welcome respite from mists and rain. Though I hadn't forgotten Ian's remarks about the uselessness of words, I smiled at him when he woke up. I had lain for several minutes, admiring his sleeping face, his strong jawline, his ears, close-set to his head. When his eyes opened, I had been fingering a lock of hair that had fallen on his forehead.

He drew me into an embrace. A kiss followed that awakened my desire. We made love, and I forgave him his failure to adore words as I did. He was a water man, a man of pulsing rhythms who understood the science of molecules and ocean tides.

Before he left, he surprised me by handing me a lover's knot woven from sea grasses. "I made this for you while I was waiting for results of a water test."

"When did you learn to do this?" I asked.

He smiled. "In grade school, we used to make them for our girl-friends."

I teased him. "Am I your girlfriend?"

"More than that," he said.

He kissed me and left. Did he mean he loved me? I twirled in a circle like a schoolgirl, caught in the throes of first love. Catching sight of myself in the dresser mirror, I stopped. What was I thinking? There was no way I'd live in the Kincaid house with his strange sisters! I'd always chafe at the biases and rhythms of the town. Where did that leave Ian and me?

I glanced at the clock. Only forty minutes to get to class. Hurriedly, I showered, dressed in navy slacks, a white blouse, and sandals, and drove to the campus.

Before I introduced my students to Amen Jones' poems, I read the partial poem I'd found days ago on the gazebo floor.

> *Lady Fair, Lady Fair, you cannot dispute*
> *Your bones are gnarled like pine tree roots.*
> *Who is your...*

"This poem has a lovely beginning," I said. "I wanted to return it to the author."

No one admitted to writing it. Baffled, I folded it and put it in my purse. Perhaps Amen left it on the floor, or Constance. Lady Fair could refer to Goddess. Her maiden name was Faire. Did *gnarled bones* mean *mixed race*? Goddess was obviously of mixed race. Or did Lady Fair refer to a white woman, like June Whitehall, who would be devastated to find out African blood ran through her veins.

I turned back to my students and handed them copies of Amen Jones' poems. The verses were short; it did not take long to read them through.

"Taken as a whole," I said, "what do the poems say?"

"They seem to be linked together except for the last one."

"The poet moves from the goddess Astarte to a living, breathing woman."

"Number nine. I'm confused by *Pave my Milky Way/ Out of the root cellar.*"

"Maybe the root cellar is a grave."

"Who's the screaming duck?"

"I like the way the poet pairs biblical language like *chariots of fire* with *Milky Way*, and country expressions like *velvet skin, like a hound's ear* with a sophisticated word like *tiara*."

"I like *Did you comb the night into your hair...*"

For the duration of the class, students analyzed the poems. When they were done, they begged to know who the poet was. There seemed to be no reason not to tell them.

"His name was Amen Hotep Jones. He grew up around here. I met him when teaching a poetry class."

At five o'clock, students left the gazebo. One returned.

"Can we look at the eleventh poem?" she asked.

Moon mother, yank on the cow's horn.
I need to chew on it like a bone.
Betelgeuse, Sirius, Vega,
Come to me at midnight.

"What do you see?" I asked.

"The cow's horn is a fertility symbol," she said. "Astarte ruled the spirits of her dead children, which were stars in heaven. She wanted the stars to come out at midnight."

Raise my people.

Amen's words when he appeared to me on Death Island. I now saw a new meaning to the poem. Amen had called on the spirits of the dead to lead his people. I thanked the student for her help.

I sat for a while, looking out at the Sound. Gulls circled. Sailboats gracefully skimmed the water. A motorboat crested a wave and headed out to the ocean. Intermittently, the sound of hammering erupted from the park where workers were shoring up benches and erecting kiosks for dozens of Creightons who would be attending the reunion tomorrow.

Goddess and Pastor Mungo stopped by as I gathered up my books. I invited them to sit down.

"I thought you'd be here," said Goddess. "The other night at your place, I started to tell you about Drake and Isabella, and then we got onto the parable. I never finished."

"Yes," I said quickly. "Please tell me."

Settling herself on the wooden bench, she turned to me. "Isabella was Old Peter's only daughter. She loved Drake, one of her father's slaves. They ran away and hid out in the swamp for nearly a year. Twins were born to them, a girl and a boy."

Here was the meaning of the third Astarte poem.

Your twin appeared in the moonlight
So like you so not. Her utterances
Were the sound of a cannon.
Where do you keep your pain on Sundays?

"The boy was dark like Drake," Goddess went on, "but the girl was light-skinned. When Old Peter caught up with them, he captured

Drake, and later, burned him at the stake. What was left of him, he tossed in the river. He cut off Isabella's feet for running away, and left her and the boy in the swamp, where they died. Black folks buried them on Death Island. Old Peter took the girl to raise."

The horrible scenes played out in my mind. My God! What barbarity! Were the times really that savage? Or had Peter Creighton been a madman?

After a moment, I asked, "Was Drake burned on a Sunday?"

"Right after church services. We hold a special remembrance of him on Sundays."

"What happened to Isabella's daughter?" I asked.

"Old Peter Creighton married her off to a planter."

It took a few seconds for the ramifications of Drake's daughter married off to a planter to sink in. If she had issue, his blood would flow through Cherapee County like the Orchy River and all its tributaries.

"Did she have children" I asked.

"Twelve, like the tribes of Israel," said Pastor Mungo.

"Were they light-skinned?" I asked.

"It's said some were, but some were dusky," replied Goddess. "Everybody was afraid to challenge Old Peter, so the whole county pretended they were white. They married white."

"Drake's blood unites blacks and whites. Is this what the parable is about, Pastor Mungo?"

"Partly."

I turned to Goddess. "What was Isabella's daughter's name?"

"Folks say her given name was Astarte. Peter called her Petronelle."

I'd seen the statue of Astarte in the soil surrounding Isabella's grave. Goddess had said Amen placed it there. Isabella had been buried with her son, but not her daughter. Amen had sought to bind both children to their mother by adding the representation of Astarte.

"Are you one of Petronelle's descendants?" I asked Goddess.

Goddess nodded. "I'm a Creighton through both parents. Johnny Parks chased Mama down when she was just fourteen."

"There are a lot of double-Creightons," said Pastor Mungo.

"The reunion was always for the so-called 'pure blood' Creightons, those descended from Peter's son, William," said Goddess. "Petronelle's children were always left out. This year, we're invited too. I'm thinking the reunion committee is opening up about race."

"Who's on the reunion committee?" I asked.

"Locally, Mrs. Whitehall. Others, from Virginia."

I looked quickly at Goddess. June Whitehall did not appear to be a liberal-thinking person.

"Are you going?" I asked.

"I thought I might. I plan to dress up, you know, be as grand as those Creightons coming down from Virginia, and, of course, Mrs. High-and-Mighty Whitehall."

"You mustn't go," I said.

"I don't think she should either," said Pastor Mungo.

Anger flared in Goddess's eyes. "Why are you telling me that? I'll be okay. I'll be seated at a table with the rest of them."

She got up to take her leave. Pastor Mungo stood up, his face a study in alarm. I hoped he would dissuade her from attending.

I sat alone in the gazebo, searching for a connection between the murders and Drake's slave blood running through Cherapee County families. I strained to remember the lineage chart Bo had drawn. Old Peter had one son. His descendants, if they did not wed Petronelle's, would be the "pure bloods."

Were Lavinia Dawson, Dorothy Creighton, Monty Dodd, and Johnny Parks all descendants of Petronelle?

Then I remembered the Creighton who was running for governor—Luther Vance. If he were descended from Petronelle, he might want to suppress the story of Isabella and Drake. Surely, he wouldn't murder people to achieve that end.

Or would he?

I had a burning desire to read Bo's notes again. Shoving books into my briefcase, I hurried to my rental car and drove to the sheriff's department. Specifically, I wanted to look at what Bo had written about X—a person he'd been unable or reluctant to name, even in code.

Verlie Post was out, but one of the deputies brought Bo's binder from a locked room. I sat at a table and opened the binder. One entry said X = the drawing of a tree. What did Bo mean? It made no sense to me, but apparently, it had made sense to Bo. His fondness for acrostics showed in X + (picture of a half camera) + (a window). I stared for several seconds and then it came to me. The window was a pane of glass. Half a camera was *cam*. *Campaign*. X had to be Luther Vance, who was running for governor. Or it could be someone connected with the campaign. But was Vance a killer? Bo also used lower case x's. Were X and x two different people? In a margin, Bo had written x = NBAHT.

Oh, Bo, I sighed, why couldn't you have been clearer? Then I realized, when he made these notes, he may have feared for his life. One of the small x's wore a pilgrim's hat. Was Bo trying to say the killer was an official? Or a newcomer? On one page, the letters CCC were written inside a flowered wreath. Did it mean Cherapee County Creightons? Or something else?

My head began to ache. I thanked the deputy and headed home. Outside my cottage, three retreat instructors were commiserating about the murders.

"Can you believe it?" exclaimed one. "I never dreamed when I signed on, that I'd be in the midst of a crime wave down here."

"It's downright creepy," said another. "I find myself looking over my shoulder."

"And poor Bo," said the third. "Why would anyone kill him?"

I sympathized with my colleagues, then went inside to the kitchenette, where I fixed a grilled cheese and onion sandwich, and sat down to eat. Phoebe Burns called.

"We need ushers for the reunion," she said, "especially for late arrivals. Can you help?"

"I don't think so," I said.

"Oh, do usher for us, Maria. It'll show your appreciation for the Daffodil Writers Retreat. Be a good sport. The ceremonies should be over by two. If you want to come back next year, it will look good on your rating."

"No."

"Then will you at least dress in your fanciest gown and stand at the park entrance to hand out programs?"

I agreed to do that.
It was a good thing I did.

CHAPTER EIGHTEEN

The first day of the Creighton reunion broke with calm skies. I parted the curtains to look out the window. Gorgeous day! The sun had burned away the mists and the Sound shimmered like polished glass. White clouds reclined in a Monet blue sky. Still, I felt apprehensive: it was the first day of the Creighton reunion. Would people be safe?

Ian called after breakfast, asking if I'd like to go boating.

"Love to, but I told Phoebe I'd hand out programs at the reunion."

"You're going to the Creighton reunion?"

"Shouldn't you go, too? You're related."

"Bathy goes, but I hardly ever do."

"Phoebe hinted my participation was expected because the Daffodil Writers Retreat hired me for the summer."

"That's outrageous."

"I thought so too, but I might want to come back."

He didn't respond. My words had conveyed parting. Until that moment, I doubt either of us had contemplated the hard fact of my eventual leaving.

"What time will you be done?" His gone was gruffer than usual.

"The program starts at ten," I answered. "Most everything's done by two."

He was quiet for a moment. "I could pick you up then. We'd still have several hours of daylight on the water."

We said goodbye, and I selected a pale turquoise dress of silk and lace from the closet. I'd brought it in case of a formal event. Taking time with my makeup and hair, I made myself presentable.

When I arrived at the park, Phoebe was waiting at the gate with a box of programs. I took them and positioned myself next to a sign:

No Alcohol Allowed. The sunshine held. Two pink flamingoes grazed near the sea grass by the pond. In other circumstances, I might be jotting down the words of a poem.

The morning was a blaze of green. I let my eyes settle on the reunion area, noting the vases of orchids on the table and the ripple of golden streamers tied to tree limbs. The head table skirt was festooned with ivy and large crepe paper blossoms in red, white, and blue.

People arrived. Shades of the Kentucky Derby! My eyes widened as Creighton after Creighton filed onto the park grounds, women in their frilly best, men in dark suits. A sprightly grandmother wore a Dolly Varden hat—a large straw covered with peonies and lilies. Then came three twenty-somethings with fascinators pinned precariously to the sides of their heads. Goddess walked in, stunning in ivory linen and matching straw hat. Bethia Parks was in mauve, and two students from my class wore white silk. Bathsheba Kincaid wore a lilac pantsuit.

But no children. How old did one have to be to participate in the Creighton reunion?

A moment later, I overheard a conversation between two young women.

"The kids have always been able to come until this year," one said.

I looked carefully at the crowd. Who decided kids couldn't come? Had they been disruptive in previous years? My eyes lit on the officious June Whitehall. She was speaking with caterers, who had driven their van into the area where food would be served. She didn't strike me as a person who liked children.

Verlie Post and several deputies were scattered throughout the crowd. I stood quietly, feeling my heels sink into the soft ground, wishing I'd worn flats.

Ian pulled up in his truck. He was on his cell phone and didn't get out. I glanced again at June, wondering if there was a reason she had her hand in so many pots—the Daffodil Writers Retreat, buying up historical sites, the college, the reunion, the town—who knew what else? How did she have time to buy all those coordinated outfits? Was she the reason the town ran on gossip? Did she strategically plant information or misinformation? If so, why?

She wore yellow to the reunion, and since her body type was plump, resembled an overstuffed bumblebee. Darting from the serving area to the dais and back again, she finally sat down on a padded chair and arranged a stack of papers. Behind her slouched Billy Ray Parks in a baby blue suit, his cowlick slicked back. Near his feet rested a navy backpack. June turned to him occasionally and he rose to do her bidding—adding a chair to one of the tables, bringing her a doughnut and a glass of sweet tea. Had June taken him under her wing, now that his father was dead?

Luther Vance, the gubernatorial candidate, arrived with his retinue. After shaking hands with June, he started to sit down, but suddenly stopped. With Vance was a short, broad-shouldered man with thinning black hair. He wore a bespoke tan suit and a tie that shimmered money all the way to the gate where I stood. There was no chair for him. June jumped up, turned to Billy Ray, and sent him off to fetch one. He returned with one—padded, no less—and placed it next to Vance. The dark-haired man sat down. Vance sat down. His people perched behind him on metal chairs. A camera man got up to take pictures.

Camera, I thought. Pane of glass. X equals campaign.

As the last Creighton was seated, the college marching band entered in a flurry of drum beats, then tore into a Sousa march. A petite majorette in gold sequins twirled a baton. With echoes of the march in the air, a teen-aged tenor in a too-large suit stood to sing the national anthem. Feeble applause. Immediately after, a thickset man with a beard sang *Dixie*. Applause. Cheers. Rebel yells.

When the crowd quieted, June took the microphone. "Brothers and sisters, here we are again, celebrating our wonderful family."

She introduced Luther Vance and the man sitting next to him: Ivan Pora.

"Mr. Pora has business interests in Cherapee County," June chirped. "We're honored to have him join us."

The billionaire who wanted to buy Sunfish Cove.

Verlie Parks suddenly appeared at my side. "Miz Pell," he said, "have you seen anything suspicious?"

I shook my head.

"We're looking for weapons," he said. "I don't know how many of these people are carrying. At least, they don't have long guns."

"I heard kids aren't allowed this year," I said.

"That's right. Don't know whose idea that was. Previous years, the park was filled with kids. They had a special area for them over by the swings and merry-go-round." He rubbed his chin. "There's another change. This is the first time they've told people where to sit."

Told people where to sit. What did that mean?

I moved forward for a better view. "Where's Goddess Jones?"

"She's at Table 6."

Table 6 was positioned midpoint on the semi-circle, the farthest distance from the dais. Nothing seemed untoward. Goddess chatted with her brother. Then I noticed Bethia Parks and several red-headed Creightons seated at tables close to the dais.

I looked again at Goddess' tablemates. They seemed duskier than people at the other tables. I sucked in my breath. My eyes moved to Billy Ray Parks. His backpack was gone. Then I spied one just like it beneath Goddess's table, close to the end.

The Boston marathon bombers had concealed their bombs in backpacks.

Now it made sense that no children were allowed. It made sense that Petronelle's descendants were seated together and farthest from the dais. Someone wanted to kill them.

"Bomb!" I screamed. "Table 6!"

Verlie and his deputies yelled for people to leave the table, grabbed some of them and yanked them from their chairs.

The explosion came in a blinding flash; the earth shook, the terrible sound echoed for several seconds. Flames leapt; thousands of metal fragments lashed the air. Parts of the picnic table blasted upward, and a pine tree crashed to the ground. Black smoke unfurled, choking people. Many cried out as they ran. Some of the elderly ran back into the smoke. An old man tottered on his cane, howling for his wife. A metal chair knocked down a pregnant woman. My collarbone stung. I looked down. I was bleeding.

My head throbbed and as I fought off nausea, I tried to think clearly. Get people away from the site of the blast. I dragged an elderly woman across the green and shoved her against the fence. Going back for her husband, I found him wandering near the pond. At least he was safe. The wail of ambulances cut through the melee. Soon white-coated attendants were laying people on stretchers, bearing them to vehicles. The ambulances sped away. Then they were back, loading again.

Ian rushed up to me. "You're hurt," he said, hustling me to the line for the ambulance.

"I don't need to go to the hospital."

"Yes, you do." He sat down on a bench and pulled me onto the seat. "Did you see who planted the bomb?"

"The backpack was under Billy Ray Parks' chair."

He stood up to look for Billy Ray.

"There he is!" I cried, pointing to the parking lot.

Billy Ray was running toward a blue convertible. Ian caught him and took him to one of the deputies.

When he returned, I said, "June Whitehall has to be responsible for this. She seated Petronelle's descendants at one table."

"Who's Petronelle?" he asked.

His question went unanswered because another thought flashed into my mind: What if the bombing, while satisfying some sick motive for racial cleansing, was actually meant to distract from the Creighton murders? What did Monty Dodd, Dorothy Creighton, Lavinia, and Johnny Ray have in common?

"Who's Petronelle?" he asked again.

I told him.

He stared at me. "That's what this bombing is about? I've heard parts of the story before, nothing about a woman named Petronelle. My god. Where *is* June Whitehall?"

A mass of yellow chiffon was scurrying toward us.

"Behind you."

Ian turned around.

"Isn't this awful?" June cried, her eyes tearing up. "I can't imagine who would do such a terrible thing. Was anybody killed, do you know?"

"An old couple from Macon," answered Ian. "Lucille Gibbs

might lose her baby."

"How dreadful!" cried June. "Kneel with me. I want to send up a prayer for that baby."

She grabbed Ian's hand, fell to her knees, and began praying aloud. He remained standing, and when she finished, grabbed her other hand and pulled her up. Before he could speak, Goddess, her face smeared with blood, stepped out of the ambulance line and called out to June.

"Mrs. Whitehall, you're in charge of the reunion. You can't go home. You should be making sure everyone's safe."

Her words lent a surrealistic quality to the horror, and so did June Whitehall's response. She patted her hat and turned to survey the park, littered with debris from the bomb, overturned chairs, and tattered, once beautiful hats.

"Yes, of course," she said, "Isn't it strange what fear does to a person? I completely forgot my duties."

Heading for the dais, she called out, "Make sure the fire's out. Pick up those scattered programs. We can't have the town fathers calling Creightons litter bugs."

She was bending over the skinned knee of the baton twirler when Verlie Post arrested her.

"Billy Ray Parks said you told him to make the bomb," said Verlie.

She scowled at the sheriff. "You can't believe a word that rapscallion says. How would I know how to make a bomb?"

My last sight of June that day was when she stepped into a county car to be borne away to the county jail. I'd lost my place in the ambulance line. Ian said he would take me to the hospital.

"Wait!" Someone spoke into the microphone. Seth Creighton. He had shed his ragged clothes and was dressed in a suit.

"Fellow Creightons," he said, "we planned to meet for two days. Someone disrupted our sacred gathering with hatred and violence. Don't let them win. For three hundred years, our family has come together. Workers will clean up this mess and we'll have a good day tomorrow. The sun will shine again. Come back tomorrow at ten."

A few feeble cheers.

Ian drove me to the hospital where we waited two hours until a doctor was free. She pulled out bits of metal from my shoulder, cleaned and dressed my wounds, and gave me a prescription for pain pills. I told Ian I wouldn't need the pills, so we didn't go to a pharmacy.

We were on our way to a corner tavern when Verlie Post drove up.

CHAPTER NINETEEN

The sheriff waved a document in our faces. He'd obtained a search warrant for June Whitehall's house and garage.

"Ms. Pell," he said, "I'm not sure what all I'm looking for besides evidence that Billy Ray built a bomb in her house. You've been privy to Bo Bennett's notes. Your eyes might latch onto something right away. Please come with me."

"I'm coming too," said Ian.

We climbed in the county car and rode to June's antebellum home in the center of town. Surrounding the property was a high wrought-iron fence. The sheriff drove in through the main gate and parked in the circular driveway.

"Is there a Mr. Whitehall?" I asked.

"June ran him off thirty years ago," answered Verlie.

We went up the steps and Verlie rang the doorbell. An elderly servant dressed in a shiny black suit appeared.

"Miz Whitehall is at the park," he said.

"What's your name?" asked Verlie.

"Mose Chesterton. I'm her butler."

Post held up the search warrant. "Your employer is under arrest. I'm looking for anything that will link her to a bomb."

Mose Chesterton backed away. "I don't know nothing about a bomb."

"Try the basement," Verlie said to his men.

The sheriff and Ian also headed for the basement. I followed them through a heavy oak door into the kitchen and down a flight of stairs. Verlie switched on the lights and there, in front of a three-legged stool, was a large funnel, a can of nails, and a small pile of black powder. Verlie gave instructions to his deputies to collect the evidence and we went back upstairs.

Mose huddled in the vestibule.

"Where does Mrs. Whitehall keep her papers?" I asked.

"I reckon her study would be a good place to look."

He led me upstairs to a room papered in pink roses and hung with white dimity curtains. On both sides of the window were glass etageres holding wide-skirted Dresden maidens, white geese, and black-booted shepherds. June's roll-top desk was painted pink. The slatted wooden cover was open. A quick glance revealed orderliness—no loose papers.

"Does she have a safe?" I asked.

Mose pointed to a portrait of a gentlemen in a ruffled shirt. "Behind Colonel Whitehall."

Lifting the portrait, I exposed a safe.

I looked at the butler. "I don't suppose you know the combination."

"Matter of fact, I do. She told it to me because she kept forgetting what it was."

He unlocked the safe and I opened the door. The first things I saw were six copies of the *Annals*. June had been stealing them. I moved them aside and found several folders beneath. The top one was labeled *Creighton Family*, and contained a list of family members, names and addresses, and trees of progenitors, of whom there were two: William and Isabella. Someone had tracked Isabella's descendants over a period of three hundred years. Scanning the pages, I saw Ian's name. He was descended from William. If none of his ancestors married into Isabella's line, he was white all the way through. I wondered if that would please him.

Inside a folder labeled *Miscellaneous,* I discovered a manila envelope with Amen's name on it. The heading of the first document was *Slaves Executed by Order of Plantation Owners*. Attached were pages of lists of slaves, their crimes, death dates, and names of executioners. I found the entry I was looking for:

Drake Theft of Seed Creighton Ptn Burned at stake B. Bigger 1710

I saw the irony in Drake's crime: Isabella had been Peter Creighton's seed.

This was Amen's research. He had dug through old court records for this data. *The Annals of Cherapee County* did not contain the information presented on these pages. But where was the parable?

Shuffling through the envelopes, I passed over one with *Sunfish Cove* slashed in black marker, and found the parable: *The Holy Family of Cherapee County*. Trembling, I read it through. When Ian came upstairs, I handed it to him. He read it, folded it, and put it in his jacket pocket.

"Give it back," I said, alarmed.

"I have use for it."

"You mustn't destroy it."

"What do you think of me?"

His voice was so soft I barely heard it. He gave me a hard look, and I lowered my head, unable to meet his gaze. Later, I would know that in that moment, I'd done something unforgiveable.

We went downstairs. I took the contents of the safe with me and sat on the living room sofa to look through the envelope marked *Sunfish Cove.*

"The sheriff wants you to go to the garage," said Mose.

We went to the garage.

* * * * *

The old stable, several yards across the courtyard, had been converted into a garage. When we entered, the sheriff was looking at the inside of a lime green car. On the front, was the word, *Bonra*. It was the car that chased me up Highway 168.

"I can't believe it was June Whitehall who nearly drove me off the road," I said.

Verlie turned to me. "Billy Ray admitted he was behind the wheel. June wanted him to scare you. She thought you were nosing into things that were none of your business."

"As for the car," the sheriff continued, "Billy Ray said she won it in a raffle down in Charleston. She thought it too flashy to drive around."

"Wasn't the raffle sponsored by one of Luther Vance's supporters?" asked Ian.

"Could the sponsor have been Ivan Pora?" I asked. "Russian car, Russian billionaire."

Verlie Post rubbed his chin. "I bet so. June didn't want to advertise her connection with the man wanting to buy up Sunfish Cove."

I opened the *Sunfish Cove* envelope. Inside was a list of its owners. Lavinia Dawson's name was at the top, then Dorothy Creighton, Monty Dodd, and Johnny Parks. Ian's was halfway down the page, just above Alberta Jones and Lanny Faire. Stapled to the list was a copy of a personal check made out to June Whitehall for five hundred thousand dollars and signed by Ivan Pora.

"This should be enough evidence to convict June Whitehall of murder," I said, handing the copy to the sheriff. "Pora wants Sunfish Cove and he paid June Whitehall a half-million dollars to get it for him. She couldn't talk some of the owners into selling, so she began killing them off. Four victims are on the list, and Goddess and her brother were at the table that blew up."

"Let's see that list." Ian grabbed it from my hand. "There are thirty-two owners. Some of us are major investors, but we offered shares at a lower cost so there would be plenty of community involvement. A lot of the hold-outs for the sale were seated at Table 6."

"Why would Pora pay that much money to get the cove?" asked Verlie.

Digging deeper into the envelope, I found a document marked *Report of Seismic Tests,* and scanned the first line.

"There's oil in Sunset Cove," I said.

Ian reached for the report and read the first page.

"Verlie," he said, "Pora sent in an outfit from Texas to conduct tests last summer. Must've done it at night. No one knew." He looked at me. "At the state level, someone must have known. Luther Vance might be in on this with Pora."

"If June accepted money to do away with owners who refused to sell, who did the murders?" cried Verlie. "Billy Ray is a misguided teenager, not a killer. I can't see June Whitehall climbing two floors to shoot Monty Dodd."

"A woman is involved," I reminded them. "The woman who tried to shoot me."

Depression hit me. June had scented her house with lily-of-the-valley, and I was slightly nauseated. Her living room, with violet carpet and walls, and cream accoutrements added to my discomfort. I thought of the bomb that had killed an old couple and threatened the life of an unborn child. June Whitehall's depravity, the bombing, Sunfish Cove, a Russian billionaire's greed for oil, possible collusion from a gubernatorial candidate, the epic tragedy of Drake and Isabella, and their little son—all filled me with unutterable sorrow. I thought of Bo, who had died because he'd stumbled on secrets.

"I need to go home," I said.

Verlie Post reached for the folders. "I'll take this to my office and look through it tomorrow."

It was nearly evening. After leaving the Whitehall house, the sheriff dropped Ian and me back at the tavern, where the pickup was parked. Neither of us was in a mood to talk. We had one drink apiece and then my chest began to hurt. I wished for the pills I'd refused and swallowed a Tylenol from my purse.

"What do you do after you've seen someone try to blow people to bits?" I asked.

My tone was slightly manic. Ian stared at me, no hint of empathy. Did he see me as mocking?

I was expressing pain.

"Let's go out on the water," he said.

We drove to the Sound and borrowed a sailboat. The waters were a dusty blue, indistinguishable from the sky. I leaned back, gazed at the darkening horizon. Did I see a thunderhead in the east? Sea breezes fanned my face, cooled my shoulders, my arms. The pain in my chest lessened as I relaxed. It was good to be out on the water, away from the suffering town. Ian sat at the helm, glowering, alone with his thoughts.

I considered moving closer to him, touching him. I had no doubt that he loved his socially stratified community, with its visceral ties to a romanticized past. Yet he was also part of a forward-thinking group that reduced shares so poorer folk could own Sunset Cove. I studied his profile; strong chin, straight nose, his hair ruffling in the wind. It broke my heart to think of leaving him. I did not try to comfort him. I needed strength for myself.

After an hour on the water, we returned to the dock and drove home. My wounds began to pain me again and I took another Tylenol. Later, I roused Ian from his sleep to make love. Strangely, I was wild for him.

* * * * *

Morning, with unbearable humidity, came too soon. I remembered my commitment to hand out programs on the second day of the reunion. Ian and I finished breakfast, then kissed goodbye. He left to do paperwork before returning to the park. I dressed in a navy sheath, no hat.

I arrived at the park gate at 9:30, and ducked into a park gazebo to wait out a freshet of rain. Sunshine followed. Now the chair seats were wet. Who would wipe them off? June was sitting in a jail cell, unable to direct park staff.

The people came, not as many as before. Some had gone home. The gubernatorial candidate and his minions didn't return. Nor did Ivan Pora. People were subdued, wary. They had toned down their wardrobes—there were few frothy hats. Seth Creighton sat alone at the head table, and I assumed he would conduct the meeting.

Ian came to stand beside me. He'd changed into a navy-blue suit.

"Look who's joining Seth on the dais," he said.

Pastor Mungo was shaking hands with Seth.

"Maybe this is going to be a 'come to Jesus' meeting," he added, cryptically.

Seth Creighton called the meeting to order.

"Brothers and sisters," he intoned, "the sheriff says June Whitehall was behind the bombing yesterday. I never cottoned to June, but it's hard as all-get-out to think the woman who's arranged our reunions all these years would want to kill us. The bomb that went off killed our cousins from Macon and the unborn child of one of our young women. Let's take a moment to remember them."

We bowed our heads.

When the moment was over, Seth cleared his throat. "Last night, I thought of trying to persuade y'all to end these yearly get-togethers, but this morning, the sun rose as always, the Sound was peaceful as usual, and I realized that was a bad idea. Our reunions should continue."

A smattering of applause.

"Let me tell you why," Seth continued. "It's tradition, and the South lives and breathes tradition. Once I was like that, loving our traditions. When my father disinherited me, I went to rack and ruin, abandoned my law practice, went begging on the streets. I felt cast out. I felt tradition had let me down, and maybe it had." He paused. "But from the position of outcast, I was able to see things I hadn't seen as an insider. I saw our past clearly, the good deeds and hard work that brought us prosperity, and the bad practices that brought us to ruin. I mean our curse, slavery, and its after effects."

Chins lifted. I heard the rumble of discontent.

"Yes," said Seth, "I said the word. Slavery. It is an abominable thing to enslave people. Our forefathers erred grievously by participating in that evil enterprise. I know the climate was thought to be too hot for our Celtic kinsmen to go out picking cotton and tobacco, but they could have adapted."

Looking out over the crowd, Seth said, "Slavery is at the bottom of the race hatred we have in Cherapee. Don't let anybody tell you different."

The audience went silent.

He shook his head. "The people sitting at Table 6 were the descendants of a slave named Drake and Isabella Creighton, through their daughter, Petronella. All of you over the age of fifty know that story because it ran through the county like wildfire during the civil rights era. For you younger folks, it is this: Old Peter Creighton's daughter, Isabella, ran off with a slave and lived with him in the swamps. Old Peter got a posse together and went in after them. Took him a while to find them, but he did. He cut off Isabella's feet and left her to bleed to death. He burned Drake at the stake. There were two babies. The dark-skinned boy died with his mother. The girl was white, so Old Peter took her to raise. He named her Petronella, after himself. She married a white man. Their children had black blood running through their veins. Thus, we have the so-called tainted Creighton line."

A gasp went through the crowd.

I shifted in my seat. Obviously, Verlie Post had not shared with Seth the suspicion that the bomb was set to facilitate the sale of Sunfish Cove. But wait! What if June Whitehall had used racial strife to distract from the real reason for the bombing? I thought of the desecrated graves. Was June also behind that, wanting blacks to be blamed?

I looked for Verlie Post, wanting to share my theory with him, but Ian was making his way to the dais. I turned my head to follow him.

He grabbed the microphone. "Most of you know me," he said, "but for those who don't, I'm Ian Kincaid. I live outside Cherapee with my sisters in a two-hundred-year-old house handed down from our forefathers."

"I knew your grandpa," shouted an old man.

"Blessings on you," said Ian.

This was a side of Ian I had never seen. He was a natural in front of a crowd. *He* should have been the gubernatorial candidate.

"I have a story to read to you," he said. "Some folks call it a parable, and I suppose it is because it teaches a lesson. It's called *The Holy Family of Cherapee County*. It was written by a poet, Amen Hotep Jones."

The crowd murmured. Local people knew Amen.

"It's told in first person," said Ian. "The narrator has wandered into the swamps..."

On a journey through the swamps, I interrupted an old woman, who was praying in front of a carving of a father, mother, and two swaddled infants. A voodoo idol, I thought, for the old woman was black and her hut was filled with fetishes I could not ascribe to the Christian faith. When I asked who the idol represented, she replied, Familia takatifu ya Cherapee. I understood the word familia to mean family, and of course, I knew she had spoken the name of the county where I resided. Was she speaking Swahili? "Speak English," I implored, and she complied. "The holy family of Cherapee," she said. "It is to this man and this woman people in Cherapee County owe their lives."

Now I, a white man, had lived in Cherapee County all my life, and my father before me. In fact, eight generations of my family had lived there. She could not have meant me.

I asked her to tell me about the holy family. She sat on a stool and invited me to sit in a chair made of cypress logs. Following, is the story from her lips.

"There once lived Drake, a descendant of African kings, who had been kidnapped and brought to America as a slave. He found love with Isabella, a daughter of European kings. Because his skin was as black as a moonless sky, and hers was the color of mists, their love was forbidden. They ran away to the great swamp and soon, twins were born to them—a boy, whom they named Enki, after a Sumerian god, and a girl whom they called Astarte, after a Middle-Eastern goddess.

Within the year, the family was discovered by a hate-filled mob and all were killed except Astarte, who was taken to live in her maternal grandfather's household, and renamed Petronelle. Also in the household lived her uncle, his wife, and their son Jacob, who was the same age as the orphaned girl.

Petronelle and Jacob were schooled together, played together, and were always in each other's company. Eventually, they married and had twelve children, all of whom robustly populated the county."

The old woman concluded her story and looked at me. "Drake and Isabella and their children are considered holy, not merely our own Adam and Eve, but exemplars of interracial tolerance."

She was obviously learned and I asked to know her story. "You need know only that I was a disciple of Dr. King, and that when he was murdered, I left the world to live in this swamp."

I went away from this encounter with expanded knowledge. I had known the old story of Drake and Isabella, their doomed love and tragic end, but had not considered the significance of the surviving child, Astarte, who came to be known as Petronelle, with her mixture of African and European blood. I knew that in addition to Isabella, Old Peter Creighton had three sons, and assumed the pure-blood Creighton line had come down from them. But William was the only son to survive into adulthood. He had but one child—

Jacob—and he had married Petronelle. Since I was a descendant of William, through Jacob, Drake's African blood ran through my veins.

Ian stared into the crowd, which had grown silent. No doubt, many were visualizing their family trees.

A tall gentleman with a mane of white hair stood up. "I have Old Peter's bible. It says Jacob Creighton married someone named Nell."

"That's Petronelle," said Ian.

"Who'd you say wrote that parable?" demanded a woman.

"Amen Jones," answered Ian. "He was a black farmer who lived in Cherapee County. Maybe your brother."

"Amen!" shouted Pastor Mungo.

Ian folded the pages of the parable. "This parable is about all of us. Our lineages are whip-sawed and crisscrossed. We're brothers and sisters, all of us. Not one of us could produce a lily-white pedigree."

"I ain't no brother to niggers," yelled a man.

A shot rang out.

I thought it was a car backfiring. Ian clutched at his throat and fell, dragging the Confederate flag down with him.

"Ian!" I screamed, and ran toward him.

A man pushed me out of the way, shouting he was a doctor. He bent over Ian. What did he say? "He's gone. Bullet went into his brain." Did I hear those words or imagine them? My stomach clenched; it was as if I had swallowed a heavy stone. Crazed hornets filled my head. The doctor stood. I sat down on the ground, cradled Ian's head, feeling the warmth of his blood pouring over my hands. How could he be dead if he was still warm? Was there hope? Was the doctor wrong? But then I wiped the blood from his beautiful turquoise eyes and saw them staring sightlessly at the sky. I closed his lids, bent, and kissed his lips.

"Maria, get up. Come with me." It was Phoebe Burns.

"Ian's gone."

"Yes, dear, he's gone. Get up. The ambulance is coming to take him away."

"Away?" I couldn't comprehend. He was already gone. Away.

Then I thought I wanted to be rooted in that place, holding my darling's body. I saw us carved into a sculpture like the Holy Family, one slain by the same kind of hatred that had killed Drake and Isabella.

Phoebe shook my shoulder. "Bathsheba is coming. You must get up."

Bathsheba Kincaid screamed, "You! Get away from my brother!"

I placed Ian's head on the ground. Bathsheba flung herself on his body. Phoebe put her arm around my shoulder and led me away.

"Wait," I said, "I didn't tell him goodbye."

We both turned. Bathsheba had covered Ian's body with her own.

"Another time," said Phoebe.

CHAPTER TWENTY

Phoebe drove me home. I cleaned myself in the shower, crawled into bed, and wrapped myself in sheets that had covered Ian and me only that morning. His scent was still on the pillow, and like the whipped bitch that I was, I rubbed my nose in it. Edging down the mattress, I buried my lips against the stiffened spot where his seed had spilled out of me. How could he be dead? His seed was still inside me.

Then I realized I didn't know who shot him. Reaching for my cellphone, I requested the number of the Cherapee County Sheriff's Department. The number flashed on my screen and I tapped it into the phone. No one answered. Who else could I call? Phoebe? I got her voice mail. My exertions tired me and I lay back on the pillows to sleep.

At midnight, I woke, worrying about my class. The retreat was nearly over—only three more days. Though I had outlines for the next sessions, I had no heart to teach. I felt too fragile. Could Phoebe find a replacement for me? If not, what would I do?

I felt the loss of Ian so keenly that for one mad moment, I considered joining him in death. Could lovers find each other in the netherworld? I supposed it would depend on whether their spiritual paths connected. Closing my eyes, I fell into a half-sleep, envisioning Ian stepping onto an endless bridge, silvered and multi-tiered, providing many passages to eternity. Mists rose to comfort him. Falls must have been nearby, for I heard the sound of tumbling water. He seemed reluctant to move on. An angel, whose head and robe were illumined by a soft glow, stretched out its hand to guide him. Ian backed away. When the angel spoke to him, Ian hesitated, then followed. I slept deeply, knowing he was safe.

* * * * *

Phoebe called the next morning. "Sorry I couldn't call you back last night," she said. "I met with some of the retreat planners and didn't get home until eleven. Some of the students went home. I don't blame them. Cherapee County has lost its idyllic charm."

"Who shot Ian?"

"Gowdy Smith," she said. "He's a Klan member—though I don't know if the Klan was behind the shooting."

The Klan? If she had said the Mongol hordes, I couldn't have been more disoriented. I ran to the bathroom and vomited. Then I lay on the sofa, weeping, dozing, and watching TV reruns. How egocentric the *Seinfeld* characters were! Did anyone care that Elaine had to ride in coach, while Jerry lived it up in first class? I was more in the mood for *Mash*, with its sad irony.

Phoebe came after work, bringing a container of vegetable soup from the college cafeteria. She had found a substitute to teach my class.

"That's a relief," I said.

"Ian's funeral is Wednesday." She wrung her hands. "Poor Maria. I didn't invite you here to have your heart broken."

I couldn't help it. I laughed. Phoebe looked alarmed and patted my hand. She left shortly after.

That night, Constance Creighton appeared in my dreams. She wore a black dress. Her hair was loose, hanging past her waist.

"When I died, my wee bairn died too," she told me. "I hoped he would be with me, but I cannot find him. It is a terrible thing."

I awoke, horrified. Why wasn't Constance's baby with her? What kind of afterworld takes a mother and an infant and doesn't put them together? Tearing off my blanket, I paced the floor, weeping over Constance's fate, her baby's fate.

It dawned on me that I was she and Ian was her baby.

The quiet ticking of the clock was ear-splitting. Removing it from the nail, I shoved it onto a pantry shelf, toppling an open box of raisin-bran. I heard the crackle of the cereal under my feet, felt the knuckles of hard little raisins as I walked away. I'd clean up the mess in the morning.

There was no moon. I searched for it through the panes of the French doors. A shaft of light from the street lamp shone on the metal pole and the grass below. I opened the doors and went out onto the small concrete patio. A breeze brushed the leaves on a nearby oak. The fog horn groaned.

I conjured Ian. His back was to me. He wasn't comprised of pulsing pixilation, so I knew I was imagining him.

I spoke to him: "You came into my life for such a short time and now you've gone before I could fully understand you. You were my Cavalier, my waterman, someone who knew the tides better than I knew Pindar's odes. Why did you come into my life? What did you teach me that I need to know?"

His image vanished in the darkness. I felt the damp and lifted my face heavenward. Did the barrier island, with its fog and rain and sometimes intolerable sunshine weave a spell? Was I affected by the ocean vastness, the incessant churning of waves?

In my midwestern home, nature didn't absorb me. Though there was a river and wooded areas and a few lakes, I lived in a townhouse with neighbors, some friendly, some not. There were manmade creations: sidewalks, flower gardens, and mailboxes. The weather usually did not dominate, but here, in Cherapee County, the weather was mood.

In Cherapee, I had loosed my tiger, enthusiastically spreading my legs for a man whom I hardly knew. I would have done so even if Mathieu had not cheated on me. I sucked in my breath sharply, realizing how tentative my hold on reasonable behavior had been. And then I smiled.

For too long, I had lived a circumscribed life—obedient daughter hiding my excursions into the spirit world, diligent scholar, poet who labored over word choice and meter, partner to Mathieu. Ian was my liberation. I had no doubt my poetry would change.

Returning to the cottage, I poured myself a glass of claret and toasted Ian.

CHAPTER TWENTY-ONE

Fresh from the dewy hill, the merry year
Smiles on my head, and mounts his flaming car;
Round my young brows the laurel wreaths a shade,
And rising glories beam around my head.

Sometimes I felt like reading William Blake. This was one of those times. The poet had an other-world frame of mind, which expanded his poetry, as well as his art. He also claimed kinship with the spirit world, conversing with his late brother Robert. This was not a time to read Olds, Plath, or even Whitman.

I was reading Blakes's "The Little Black Boy," when Mathieu called. "Maria, I'm back from Peru. When are you coming home?"

"Soon," I said.

"You have to prepare for your university classes. A letter from your dean has come. Shall I open it and read it to you?"

"No," I said.

"It might be important. What's the matter with you?"

"I've been unwell. Sinus trouble."

"Have you seen a doctor?"

"Yes," I lied.

"I really think you should cut short your time there and come home where I can take care of you."

"So kind of you, Mathieu."

A pause. "Did I hear sarcasm in your tone?"

"Is that what you thought you heard?"

"I hope not. I love you, Maria, and want you here with me."

"I'll be home in a few days," I said. "There are some things I need to do first."

I ended the call.

I couldn't deal with Mathieu until Ian was buried.

* * * * *

Wednesday. Ian's funeral. Veils of fog. Phoebe came by to get me and we drove to a white clapboard church on top of a hill surrounded by loblolly pines—the Methodist Church, attended by generations of Kincaids. We stepped into the vestibule. Floral arrangements flanked the south wall. I looked for the urn of white roses I'd ordered the day before and found it wedged between a fern from the Cherapee State Bank and a basket of chrysanthemums from the sheriff's department. Phoebe and I went into the nave and found seats in a back pew. When a group of people dressed in black filed in, she nudged my elbow.

"Gowdy Smith's family," she whispered.

I stared at the Smiths. Three men, two women. The men were lean and bearded; one woman was obese with gray hair; the other, younger, brunette, her right arm in a sling. Heads lowered, they moved noisily down the aisle and sat in a pew two rows in front of us. In their wake, they left hostile vibrations.

"Why are they here?" I muttered to Phoebe.

"Maybe they want forgiveness for Gowdy," she whispered.

Forgiveness? I didn't think so. The brunette turned to look at me before sitting down. "That's Gowdy's wife, Shirley," whispered Phoebe.

Shirley Smith reached for a hymnal with her good arm. In doing so, her sleeve inched up to reveal an eagle tattoo.

Bo's killer.

She was also the person who shot a hole in my pillow. I had broken her arm with the poker.

A sound erupted from me—guttural, animalistic. I stood, searching for Verlie Post. The Smith woman heard me and turned to stare. Fear widened her eyes.

"Do sit down," Phoebe said irritably, pulling at my arm.

"Shirley Smith killed Bo," I said.

Phoebe stared at me. "Oh dear," she said. "Wait until after the service and then tell Verlie."

Where was Verlie? My eyes searched the mourners for the sheriff. He was in the front row. I sat down. The pastor opened the service with a hymn. Then Bathsheba delivered a weeping eulogy for her brother.

"What will Judith and I do without him?" she moaned.

Phoebe wondered too. "He handled everything for them."

Verlie Post moved to the pulpit. "I asked Bathsheba and Judith if I could say a few words. Ian Kincaid was my friend. I take his death to heart. When he died, he was talking truth. We are all brothers and sisters under the skin, and we better start acting like it."

The Smith family hissed. People turned to stare at them. Deputies swarmed in, surrounded the family, and rushed them out the door.

"Doesn't seem like the Smiths were here to seek redemption for Gowdy," I observed.

"I guess not," replied Phoebe.

Sarcasm, as Mathieu often said, never became me. Why hadn't I kept my mouth shut?

The minister preached on Lazarus rising from the dead, which I thought odd. Ian wasn't going to rise from his casket. Did Ian even believe in God? I supposed he did. We'd never talked about religion. Was he a church-goer? Did he tithe? I'd never heard him curse.

"Let us trust in the Lord," said the minister, summing up his sermon.

He asked for another hymn. A clap of thunder made me drop my hymnal. It will rain on Ian's journey, I thought. We sang a hymn, full of optimism and praise for a heavenly reward, and then the minister prayed us out of the church. Running through the rain, I found Verlie Parks.

"Shirley Smith helped me carry Bo from the cottage," I said, breathlessly. "I think she shot the hole in my pillow. I broke her arm when I hit her with the poker."

"I'll pick her up," he said.

He headed toward the parking lot, speaking urgently to someone on his cellphone.

The hearse had already left. Phoebe and I got in her car and drove down a rutted dirt road to the cemetery, stopping when a cloudburst threatened visibility. I turned on the radio. Golden Oldies. Glen Campbell, singing "Galveston." We listened, not saying a word. A couple more songs—something by Peter, Paul, and Mary, and Little Richard. The rain softened to a drizzle. Phoebe started the car, driving past crabapple trees twisted by the wind. Opening my notebook, I wrote *crabapple grotesqueries*, thinking someday to put them in a poem. When we reached the cemetery gate, she parked, handed me an umbrella, and we got out of the car and made our way toward a tent, erected for Ian's family and friends.

The preacher sent Ian heavenward with a prayer and Bathsheba threw a handful of soil on top of his coffin. Judith did not make the trek to the grave; she had passed out in the undertaker's car. We all filed past Ian's grave. I'd say goodbye to him later.

Afterward, Phoebe took me back to the cottage. I sat on the bed and looked around the room. Grief, how it hurt! It blotted out the present and the future, focused only on the past. I turned on the television, listened to the news. I decided to clean the cottage, and fell to mopping, dusting, and vacuuming with a vengeance. Around six o'clock, I took off all my clothes and got in bed, pulling the blanket over my head.

CHAPTER TWENTY-TWO

Two days later, Phoebe Burns brought a copy of the county paper. The lead article told of June Whitehall's incitation of a race war to conceal the murders of Sunfish Cove owners who refused to sell to Ivan Pora. She had also paid vandals to desecrate the old Creighton graves and to burn Pastor Mungo's church. The paper did not name the Klan as the vandals, but hinted at it. According to the reporter, June had long been a supporter of the Klan, even dressing in a hooded white sheet to attend rallies. The bombing at the Creighton reunion was planned by June and carried out by Gowdy and Shirley Smith, and Billy Ray Parks.

Shirley confessed to Bo's murder. June wanted him killed because of his investigation into the murders of Dorothy Creighton and Monty Dodd. DNA from the red bandana left at Dorothy's murder scene belonged to Gowdy Smith.

"It's so beautiful here," said Phoebe. "Who knew people had such hatred in their hearts?"

"Hatred and greed," I said. "An evil mix."

Phoebe glanced at me and left. A few minutes later, Verlie Post came by.

"I read the paper," I told him. "Did June confess?"

"No," he said, "She's got herself a lawyer. Billy Ray spilled the beans. He said Gowdy carried out the Creighton killings, but June planned everything out."

"It's hard to see how Billy Ray could have worked for the woman who had his father killed."

"You didn't know Johnny Parks," said Verlie. "He was a mean son-of-a-gun."

"I wonder how much of this Bo put together."

"Quite a lot," said Verlie. "He said X = tree. I have a Russian friend in Charleston. He says *po3ra* means birch. He had Pora figured out. Thing was, he had trouble pin-pointing June Whitehall."

"He must have seen the green car."

"Billy Ray said June took the car out a couple of times during pre-dawn hours. Bo Bennett may have seen her in the car and connected her to Pora."

I shook my head. "How did Billy Ray get involved?"

"June hired him. He had just the right amount of hate in him to be of use."

"I see you tied Gowdy Smith to Dorothy Creighton's murder. What about Monty Dodd's?"

"If you recall, the wife saw a red bandana tied around the killer's neck. He didn't leave it behind."

A question had been pulsing in my mind. "Do you think anyone besides June, Billy Ray, and the Smiths were involved?"

He hesitated. "I'm not sure. I hope we've cut off the snake's head by arresting June."

We fell silent. I'm sure we both were wondering who else was out there, waiting to respond to the call to hate. A ray of sunshine dappled the tree outside my French doors. Verlie turned to look.

"A word of cheer," he said. "The People of the Ark are anchoring off Sims Island on Sundays so Pastor Mungo's parishioners have a place to worship until a new church can be built."

"Amen Jones would be pleased." I said.

Verlie Post took his leave. I sat down to re-read Amen's Astarte poems and parable. Would anyone be interested in publishing them? Without the narrative of Cherapee County, they lost some of their meaning. I toyed with the idea of providing that narrative myself and then put it aside.

I had to say goodbye to Ian and then pack to go home.

* * * * *

The crabapple trees lost their chimerical property in the sunlight. As I drove down the dirt road to the cemetery, I thought how rain and mood had maligned the trees on the day of the funeral. Parking next to the gate, I followed a pebbled path to Ian's grave. His monument had not yet been erected. I envisioned it in a stonemason's shop with his name partially carved. A metal nameplate marked his grave. Urns of flowers, most of them wilting, flanked the fresh-turned soil. To his right was a double headstone etched with the names of James and Lucinda Kincaid—probably, his parents. He had never spoken about them, except to say that his father had planted a soybean crop that failed.

I knelt down, knowing I'd never return, and searched my mind for poetic phrases to mark the occasion. I was never as glib speaking as I was with a pen in my hand or my fingers on a keyboard. Where were my images?

There had been a mis en scene—the climate, the ocean, colonial backstory, old resentments. Heat tempted the body like a warm bath, breezes stroked the imagination, and the limpid fog created mystery and a place to hide. Cherapee County held death closely, so there was a mythic veil separating the present from old stories of sin and redemption. Religiosity was lived out. Witness the *Ark*, a concept which had floated from shore to shore to save souls for three hundred years. Keeping the old houses where saints and sinners labored and loved. Though an outsider, I had exercised my own spiritual gifts to gain a sense of the past. When a handsome Cavalier appeared, I could do little but succumb.

I took the love knot he'd made me and buried it deep in the earth.

> *Waterman, my Triton,*
> *Messenger of the sea, rivers, and lakes,*
> *What a lovely fate to have known you.*

I took my leave, hoping time would give me the words to honor him as he deserved.

EPILOG

It's been a year since Ian died. I've rented a cottage on the coast of Ireland. The sea crashes against the rocks in the evenings. It is then that I sit watching the fishing boats come in. I like the look of them, appearing on the horizon in random fashion, and think of the men in their woolen caps going home to suppers of bacon and cabbage. My existence is simple, like theirs.

I've often thought about the spirit of Constance Creighton, which has not appeared to me since leaving Cherapee County. She'd told me there was something to carry out—that's why she had reached out to me. Was it to redeem her stepdaughter, Isabella, who had been so vilely treated by her father? Peter Creighton had tried to strike her name from history. Amen Hotep Jones had resurrected her, showing her to be the Nile of Cherapee County. From her, multitudes had come forth.

Perhaps that was what Constance had meant. If so, the mission was completed.

After leaving North Carolina, I returned home and taught for a year. Though Mathieu seemed ardent in his promises, I was in no mood to reconcile. Since we co-own the townhouse, we both continued to live there—he slept in the master bedroom and I in the guest room. We came and went as we pleased, growing farther apart.

We haven't officially separated. It seems so much trouble. We'd have to sell the townhouse, find new places to live. Too many decisions. Mathieu and I like the comfort of routine.

I was reluctant to tell him about Ian, but once I decided to write of my time in Cherapee, I knew Ian would loom large in the story. I told Mathieu about him. He was hurt, but knew he had no right to criticize me. He even shouldered the blame for my straying, saying if he hadn't become involved with his colleague, I would have remained faithful.

I'm not sure that is true.

With Goddess Jones' permission, Amen Hotep Jones' poetry was given life in a small chapbook, which included his parable. Pastor Mungo wrote the foreword.

A Cherapee County jury sent June Whitehall to prison for life. Another jury gave Gowdy Smith a death sentence for the murders of Dorothy Creighton, Ian Kincaid, and Johnny Parks. His wife, Shirley, got life for the murders of Lavinia Creighton and Bo Bennett. She had slipped into The Seabird, stolen Lavinia's pork chop, and substituted another, laced with shrimp. Ivan Pora returned to Russia. Luther Vance lost the gubernatorial election by fifty votes.

Though Phoebe invited me back to teach at the Daffodil Writers Retreat this summer, I declined. I'm enjoying my time here on the Irish coast. There are reminders of Druids all over Ireland. Some were poets. On evenings when the mists rise from the sea, I see them sitting on the rocks.

I've spoken with one of them.

The Astarte Poems

1

Velvet skin, like a hound's ear.
During the night, did honey bees sting your lips?
Did you comb the night into your hair
And is the moon your tiara?

2

When I saw you move from the timbers
I knew you were from Sidon.
I heard the tambourines,
the women singing,
and knew you were the song.

3

Your twin appeared in the moonlight
so like you so not. Her utterances
were the sound of a cannon.
Where do you keep your pain on Sundays?

4

You don't smile often.
Why not soften
The face you show to the world?
Come on, girl,
Plump up those cheek
muscles.
Don't be Moses meek.

5

Did I see you last night by the river?
Last night, by the dead pine--
the one with the owl's nest?
Was that you walking there
In a white dress that caught the moon streaming?

6

Big-hipped woman
I saw you laying in a box
A dove sitting on your head,
Your breasts peaked like stiff egg whites.

7

I'll meet you in the swamp
On high ground
Near the Big Cypress,
The one with howling knees.

Wear a light color
So you'll blend in
With the tea colored water
And foil Bigger the Bear.

8

Thunder rides
on a chariot of fire.
I die in a whirlwind.
Save me, Astarte.
Save me, Astarte.

9

Guide me, Astarte.
Show me yon way.
Light my star,
Pave my Milky Way
Out of the root cellar.

10

The duck's in the pan,
The coals are hot;
Let its screams
Resound throughout the land.

11

Moon mother, yank on the cow's horn.
I need to chew on it like a bone.
Betelgeuse, Sirius, Vega,
Come to me at midnight.

12

Water god
Thrashes around like a crazy old whale,
Tail smashing the follicles of pines,
Clay wet with blood red tears.
Who wants fins for living?

13

I behold you, woman of clay.
Your laughter is an aria of joy.
Be the sonar of love
where the river is deep.
Wake us all.
Wake us all.